Harlequin Romances

OTHER
Harlequin Romances
by JANE DONNELLY

The Intruder

by

JANE DONNELLY

Harlequin Books

TORONTO • LONDON • NEW YORK • AMSTERDAM • SYDNEY • WINNIPEG

Original hardcover edition published in 1976
by Mills & Boon Limited

ISBN 0-373-02064-3

Harlequin edition published April 1977

Printed in U.S.A.

CHAPTER ONE

FROM when she was a child Daisy Penrose had known that because she looked as though butter wouldn't melt in her mouth most of the time she could get away with murder.

She was a honey of a girl with flaxen curls and blue eyes and the proverbial peaches-and-cream complexion. Five foot nothing and slimly rounded, she looked younger than her twenty-two years, and because she was slightly short-sighted she tended to survey the world with an air of breathless vulnerability that smoothed her path no end.

The men who fell for her usually wanted to make the decisions, and were quite disappointed when they found she had a shrewd mind of her own. Most of the time they refused to believe it, so she never went short of admirers. She attracted men like bees to the honeypot, and that was lovely, and she knew how lucky she was.

This morning the sun was streaming through the windows of the Public Library where she worked. Dust motes danced in shimmering shafts, and the sun caught Daisy's softly curled hair and turned it into white gold.

She took back three books from an old lady who was a regular customer and a voracious reader, and said, 'Isn't it a beautiful morning?'

The old lady agreed that it was, and added that she was always sure of a smile when she came in here, and would Daisy help her find a nice love story? She knew the kind.

Hundreds of people used this library, but Daisy had a good memory for the tastes of those who liked to be advised, and old Mrs Parsons' heroes all had to be the brooding kind. So long as they were mean and moody Mrs Parsons was hooked, and Daisy went along the shelves hunting for stories of bad-tempered men whom she personally would not have touched with a bargepole. Mrs Parsons went off happy.

Daisy loved books, the feel and the smell of them as well as the words on the pages inside. Working among books delighted her as other girls enjoyed working in dress shops or on cosmetic counters. She got a sensuous pleasure from it, as well as the mental stimulation of being a busy librarian in a town that catered for tourists as well as residents.

In a small way she was a writer herself. She had always been imaginative, making up stories as a child, writing them down as soon as she could write. Sometimes now she got short stories published in magazines, she contributed articles to the local newspaper and she was working on a full-length book

The book was more a hobby than a serious literary undertaking. She had begun her saga of the dark lingards three years ago. Progress had been slow because she was enjoying the research, writing and rewriting with no urgency at all. If it never reached the library shelves it would become part of the family archives of Oak House, where the Lingards had lived for over four hundred years, and the Lingards were Daisy's family.

Tonight, after work, she hurried round to the offices of the *Redford Post*. It stood on a corner in the market square, once a large Victorian house, but the newspaper's offices for the last fifty years or so. Inside, the once-wide hall had been partitioned, the ground floor plan of rooms completely redesigned. But upstairs offices were still the old bedrooms, with picture rails, deep skirting boards, and open fireplaces where fires burned during the winter months.

The room for which Daisy was heading had been the master bedroom, and now housed the desks and filing cabinets of the features editorial staff. Daisy knew everyone in here, she had been taking in freelance contributions since she left school; and those who were still around—it was the end of the day—greeted her cheerfully.

Including the features editor, Margaret Cookson, any age between twenty-eight and thirty-eight, slick in a camel suit and a scarlet silk blouse, and with her dark hair in a swinging fringed bob. She had Daisy's latest article on the desk in front of her, and although Daisy had been asked to write this one she was still relieved when Margaret said, 'Yes, it's fine, just what we wanted.'

The paper often ran articles about historic homes and places in the area of their readership, and last week Margaret had said, 'Would Mr Lingard let us take some pictures of Oak House? There must be something interesting you could write about a place that old.'

'There certainly is,' Daisy had replied, 'enough to fill a book. In fact I'm working on a book around one of the family legends, and I'd love to do an article on it.' And so she had, and as she sat down in the chair facing Margaret Margaret said,

'Spooky tale. Did it really happen?'

'Everything in that article is supposed to be fact.' Five double-spaced typewritten pages contained the nucleus of the story of the dark Lingards. 'I'm having to pad it out in the book, of course.' Keeping to the facts as closely as she could, but having to invent conversations and situations because it had all happened so long ago.

There was an old sepia photograph Daisy had brought along to illustrate the article, and Margaret picked that up now with an appreciative lift to her smile. 'Very dishy,' said Margaret.

Daisy nodded, 'They all were. Dishy and dangerous.' The photograph showed head and shoulders of a young man, and although the print had faded the effect was still electric enough to make you gasp. 'But he was the last of them,' said Daisy, 'and he was killed in the hunting accident

7

in 1877.' She sighed. 'A shame, really.'

Margaret agreed, putting down the photograph reluctantly and moving her head to see if the piercing eyes followed. They did; it was a striking face even in this watered-down version. Heaven knows what the living man must have been like.

'If he'd hung on until 1880,' said Daisy gaily, 'I might have suggested he was Jack the Ripper. Can't you see that face coming at you through the fog?'

'You're prejudiced,' Margaret laughed, 'he doesn't look like Jack the Ripper to me.'

By now the three men and a woman, who were at and around the other desks, were joining in. The theatre and film critic said it wasn't a face he'd care to meet in a dark alley, but the fashion writer said she wasn't so sure about that.

'Well,' said Daisy, 'they all had pretty lurid histories—there were four of them altogether. This one was the last.'

'Maybe the next generation?' suggested the fashion reporter, and Daisy shrilled in mock indignation.

'Do you mind? That's my sister's sons you're talking about, and I promise you Alison won't produce any dark Lingards.' She smiled mischievously. 'Nor will Keith, the respectability of the line is safe with them.'

'That could be a pity,' said Margaret, and although Daisy went on smiling she was serious in saying,

'They're best as history. They made things much too lively when they were around in the flesh, and Oak House is so peaceful, everything is so beautiful there. I'm glad the black streak burned itself out.'

'Perhaps it is for the best.' Margaret Cookson had visited the old house, and Daisy's cottage in the grounds, and she recalled the black and white structure, the mullioned windows, the twisted chimneys. Even the barns and outhouses of the farm—Oak House had always been a farmhouse—were built in stone that had the patina of centuries. It was set in a village, miles from a town, in rolling countryside, and Margaret, who had a labour-saving town flat that suited her perfectly, hoped Oak House would always stay the way it was, part of the national heritage.

A weary-looking youngish man came in, toting a photographer's load, and brightened at sight of Daisy. It had been arranged that she should take Jack Brady to Oak House with her, where he would take a photograph of an oil painting of the first dark Lingard, that still hung on the dining-room wall.

'I've been at a play-school most of the morning,' he told Daisy as they walked downstairs together, 'and I couldn't get the little perishers to sit still for two seconds together. I'm about worn out.'

'You shouldn't have much trouble with this sitter,' Daisy comforted him. 'He'll be still for you.'

As she had known she was getting a lift home she had caught a bus this morning instead of coming to work in her own little car. Jack Brady's car stood in the office parking lot that had once been part of the garden, and when he pointed it out to Daisy she thought she might have recognised it because the car looked like its owner. Not old by a long stretch, but dull and dispirited.

Daisy's car was a third-hand banger, but she kept the chrome shining and the red paintwork bright, and a boyfriend who was a design artist had painted a daisy—golden centre and white pink-tipped petals—on the door. Hers was a good little car, it went like a bird, humming along, but as she took her seat in Jack Brady's vehicle she wasn't surprised to hear it splutter complainingly as he turned on the ignition.

They drove through the town and took the road in the direction of Daisy's village, and Jack said conversationally, 'Writing a book, then?'

'Yes.'

'So am I. My third.'

Daisy was impressed. 'Do you write under your own name? I work in the library, you know, I may have——'

'None of them published,' he said glumly. 'Westerns. It makes a change from wedding photographs.' The photographs that appeared in the *Post* were rarely exciting, and Jack Brady was the photographer who usually got the routine jobs. Daisy hoped he enjoyed himself writing about the old Wild West. She said,

'My book's escapism too. Not about today. It's historical, semi-documentary.'

'What's the plot?'

'Something that happened in the house I almost live in. My sister does live there, she married Keith Lingard of Oak House Farm, and back in James the First's time the young mistress of the house had an affair with a dark stranger.'

'I think I've read this book,' said Jack, but Daisy shook her golden curls at him.

'No, you haven't, and it did happen, there are records of it, letters and things. Some said he was a pirate and some said he was the devil.'

'The *devil*?' Jack turned to give her an astonished look, coasting along in the traffic that was leaving town. Daisy shrugged.

'Oh, they were always on the lookout for the devil in those days, they thought he was turning up everywhere, all over the place.' She settled herself more comfortably. 'Anyhow, there was this affair and a son was born.'

'With a patch over his eye and cloven hooves?' Jack managed a chuckle and Daisy smiled with him so that he thought what a pretty girl she was.

'No,' she said, 'with a dark visage and a crooked smile, according to the first account, and the dead image of the dark stranger. He got the house too, although there was a brother two years older.' She dropped her voice to a hoarse whisper, playing up the melodrama. 'The brother fell out

10

of a window when they were alone in a room together.'

'Did he?' said Jack. 'And you're writing about him?'

'And the others. Dark Lingards turned up from time to time. Four of them in all. I'm on Frederick the Georgian one now. He abducted an heiress and forced her to become his wife.'

'Your sister picked a rum family to marry into.' He wondered if her sister looked like her. He had seen Daisy in the office occasionally, he didn't really know her, nor anything about the Lingards, but she had a bubbling joy of life that raised a man's spirits. He felt less weary than he had done ten minutes ago.

'Oh, the Lingards are very solid country stock,' said Daisy. 'Yeoman farmers.' They were into the countryside now, and she looked out over the broad fields. It had been a lovely day and it was going to be a lovely evening, the blue sky was tinged with rosy pearl. She said, 'It's well over a hundred years since a dark Lingard was born, so I think we've seen the last of them. Now tell me about your books.'

Oak House was well back from the road, up a wide track. Farmlands spread away to the horizon and over the hills, and trees stood along the hedgerows. Daisy knew and loved every inch of this land, every tree, and as the car passed a small copse at the side of the track to the house she said, 'There's my home.'

There was a cottage, built on to a barn, backed by the spindly trees. Not so old as the house, but in Cotswold stone with a tiled roof. Red check gingham curtains brightened the windows, and a brass door knocker, shaped like a horseshoe, gleamed against the white-painted door.

'Very nice,' said Jack Brady.

Daisy thought so. She had been born in that cottage and so was Alison. The sisters were the fourth generation of Penroses to live there. Until their father died there had always been a Penrose man working on the farm, but

11

mechanisation had reduced the work force so much it didn't matter that the last of the line were girls; and that both had chosen other professions, Daisy becoming a librarian, and Alison working in a bank until she married.

When their father died, four years ago, the girls had stayed on in the cottage. Old Robert Lingard who owned the farm had always treated them as family, always approved of Alison as a future wife for Keith. There had been no obstacles to that match. From childhood the Penrose girls and the orphaned grandson of Robert's brother John had grown up together, like brother and sisters, until Alison and Keith declared themselves in love, which suited everybody. They were nearing their second wedding anniversary, and old Robert was still saying that the smartest thing young Keith had ever done was to marry Alison.

Alison now lived in the farmhouse, of course. It was ramblingly inconvenient with far more rooms shut up than were in use, and Daisy was always being urged to move in too. But she loved her cottage, and she smiled when folk said that living alone and isolated was risky.

She had two dogs, only one really counted as a protector, but the other was a good yapper, and some stout locks and bolts on doors and windows. She always felt safe in the cottage, and once you started letting fear dictate to you you could end up afraid to cross a road.

Jack Brady hadn't seen Oak House before, and he whistled as they reached it. 'That is a picture,' he said, and Daisy beamed with the pride of ownership she always felt towards this house.

Perhaps in more class-conscious days the farm workers' families were 'kept in their place', but Daisy and Alison had always called Robert Lingard 'Uncle Bob', and Daisy had run in and out of Oak House from a child, never needing to knock on a door. The house was always open to her, and long before Alison married Keith there had been a kinship, close as a blood relationship, between the Penrose girls and the boy and the ageing man who lived in the big house.

It was in the library here that Daisy's love of books was fostered. The Lingards weren't academics, but they were hoarders, and one large room was lined with shelves and hundreds of books. Unfortunately even the oldest weren't worth a great deal, but Daisy had catalogued them all, and kept them in order, and often spent wet afternoons straining her eyes reading the abominable print.

The Lingards were her family. She knew them from their pictures, from spidery signatures on the flyleaves of books, from the trunks and drawers and boxes of family papers that had accumulated through the centuries. And she couldn't remember when she had first heard the story of the dark Lingards.

She had grown up with that. It had been the thing that might reach out and grab you when you played hide and seek and found yourself alone in an unused part of the house. The room, high over the courtyard, from which the brother had fallen, had been empty from long before Daisy's day, and wild horses wouldn't have got her near the window, because if you stood there you might get pushed. Keith and Alison had always been able to make her run if, they told her, 'A dark Lingard's coming to take you away.'

Now childhood was long over, and the dark Lingards were no longer bogeys, but they still had a fascination for her. She couldn't leave them alone. She would probably be getting this book together for years yet.

All houses as old as Oak House have legends, all families going back as far as the Lingards have black sheep, but it was a proven fact that the reprobates among the Lingards looked eerily alike.

There was no portrait of one of them, just letters and a journal that numbered Roger among the dark Lingards. But a painting and a miniature and a photograph, spanning the first and the last and the Georgian one between, could al-

13

most have been the same man.

Apart from them the Lingards had an unbroken law-abiding community-serving record. But the men with the crooked smiles were the ruthless ones, an alien breed. The more Daisy delved into their records the more incredible it seemed that they could have any connection at all with Uncle Bob and Keith.

As the car drew up round the side of the house, by the stable block, Daisy pointed to a latticed window. 'That's where he fell, or was pushed,' she said, 'the top end window,' and Jack Brady found himself staring at the cobblestones, and reflecting how small that window was for a man to crash through by accident. As though this was yesterday's crime instead of happening three hundred years ago. He said,

'The place hasn't changed much, has it?'

'Not outside,' said Daisy. 'Not too much inside, except that there isn't the money about these days. There used to be horses in the stables, of course, and there were grooms and gardeners and a household staff. Now there's my sister and nanny and whoever they can get to come in and give them a hand.'

She opened a door into a flagstoned passage and two dogs came running to greet her; a perky little West Highland terrier, his rough coat snowy white and his eyes bright as black diamonds, and a very large pekingese.

The terrier went crazy, jumping up and circling round, barking in almost demented joy. The peke moved stolidly in, shouldering the terrier aside, sitting upright so that he looked like one of the Queen's Beasts until Daisy scratched the top of his head and said, 'Hello, I'm home,' then moving back without hurry while she scooped up the squirming, yapping terrier.

'Is he yours?' asked Jack.

'Yes.'

'It's not hard to tell that.' The terrier was nuzzling

14

against her neck, and she was laughing, holding her head back from its slobbery kisses. 'That's something like a welcome! Is the peke your sister's dog?'

'No, he's mine too.'

'He doesn't seem so affectionate.'

'Depends what you mean by affection,' said Daisy. 'If you hit me Woo would run like a rabbit, but Cooch there would go for your throat.'

The peke was a very big dog by pekingese standards, with broad shoulders, pugnacious jaw and unblinking eyes, and Jack Brady decided he preferred the terrier. When Daisy put down the terrier he bent to pat it, and was rewarded by a friendly wag of the tail. He didn't touch the peke. The peke's expression was not friendly.

A door from the passage opened into a kitchen where Alison Lingard was putting the finishing touches to a plate pie, fixing a pastry 'rose' and four 'leaves' on top. She wore a white bib-apron, her hands were covered in flour, and she smiled, 'I hoped I'd have time to make myself look respectable before you came. Sorry about this.'

'This is Jack Brady from the *Post*,' said Daisy. 'This is my sister Alison Lingard.' Alison had been expecting the photographer. She had intended to have the cooking done before Daisy arrived with him, but the washing machine had played up this morning. She milk-glossed the top of her pie and asked,

'Will you have a cup of tea, Mr Brady, before my sister introduces you to our skeleton in the cupboard?'

'What? Oh, you mean the dark Lingard. No, thank you, no tea.' They were good-looking girls, he thought, both of them, and fond of each other—the smiling glance they exchanged had shown that.

Alison was taller, her hair was copper red and she spoke and moved briskly, looking less of a dreamer than Daisy. Alison was a born homemaker. She had been an efficient and conscientious bank clerk, but she was a marvellous farmer's wife, good cook, good manager, good interior decorator.

Oak House was rather shabby these days; the farm paid its way, but the affluent times were over. The Lingards were poorer than they had ever been, and Alison spent as much time as she could with a paintbrush in her hand, emulsioning the fading walls. It wouldn't be her fault if the rooms were no longer bright and beautiful. She loved the place, as daisy did, and she had always loved Keith, and she asked no more of life than the chance to go on looking after her home and her family.

'I'll show you the picture, then,' said Daisy. Jack Brady followed her, admiring carving and panelling. Through one open door he glimpsed dust-sheeted furniture, but there was no smell of decay or air of neglect. That might be ahead, a place this size must be a liability, but right now it was still a home, and laughter sounded natural in it, when he looked at the painting and said,

'Seeing him, I think his brother was pushed,' and Daisy laughed.

The dining room had Victorian furniture, a long mahogany table with a dozen matching chairs around it, and a heavy carved oak sideboard almost filling one wall. The pictures were country scenes, except for the oil painting of the man. Tiny hair cracks all over gave it a mosaic effect, and the black tunic and lace collar dated it a couple of hundred years before the faded photograph Daisy had taken into the newspaper office. But this man, with the thin dark moustache and the pointed beard, had the same mocking, saturnine features. He was not smiling, but you felt that if he did it would be a crooked smile; and the dark eyes seemed to hide sinister secrets.

'He pushed him,' said Jack Brady again. His voice sounded loud, and he began to fix lights for taking his picture while Daisy sat on the table's edge, swinging feet crossed at the ankles.

16

She said, 'You think so? I've always given him the benefit of the doubt, but the dark Lingards did seem to make their own opportunities.'

'If they looked like him I'm sure they did.' He looked straight at the portrait again, and it was like it was when he was writing his Wild West tales and could outstare a gunslinger because it wasn't real. If that man had been alive Jack Brady knew he would have been scared to death of him. He shivered, although it was warm in there.

The two sisters waved Jack Brady off. Alison, without her apron now, turned to Daisy as the car disappeared and asked, 'Is he married?'

'I don't know,' said Daisy.

'You're not interested in him?' As Daisy began to laugh Alison did too and said,

'Sorry. It's just—well, you know——'

'It's just that you want me married off,' said Daisy, and Alison protested,

'No, I don't. Not until you meet the right man.' She had always known that Keith was right for her and she wished that Daisy could find the same sweet certainty. She did want Daisy married. Maybe then they would come and live in Oak House.

Alison had plans for making a self-contained flat for Daisy and her husband, that she was keeping to herself for the time being, although she knew that Keith and Uncle Bob would agree. Even if Daisy insisted on staying on in the cottage it would be better if there was a man there too. The cottage was too isolated for a girl on her own. It worried Alison, but arguing did no good. Daisy, who looked as though she couldn't say boo to a goose, could be stubborn as a mule.

'I've told you,' she was saying now, 'I won't mind being a spinster aunt.'

'Patience,' said Alison, 'all in good time.' This was a wonderful place for children, this rambling old house, fresh air and open countryside. Here children would grow strong and happy, as Alison and Keith and Daisy had done. 'And I've told you,' said Alison, 'that I shall expect some cousins for my children to play with.'

The sisters went back into the kitchen, a big comfortable room that was now used for family meals, and usually in the evenings unless there was company. Alison began to lay the table for four while Daisy helped herself to gingerbread out of the biscuit tin.

'The washer blew up this morning,' said Alison. 'I'd got it full of sheets and all of a sudden there was this bang.'

The laundry room led off the kitchen, and Daisy glanced towards the door with some trepidation. *'Blew up?'*

Alison peered into one of the saucepans, simmering on the stove, and said, 'Died on me. There was this bang and that was it, and I had to take out all the sheets and wash them in the sink and dry them outside. Good job it was a good drying day, I didn't even have Nanny to help me. She went into Woodmont with the men.'

Nanny, Miss Moreton, was all that was left of the bustling staff of the thirties. She had helped to rear Keith and the motherless Penrose girls, and although she was given to lamenting the good old gracious days she was a stalwart in the war against inflation. She shopped with an avid eye for the best buy, and she was always ready to help in Alison's do-it-yourself painting and decorating. Her regret there was that she was not surefooted enough to climb ladders these days, but within her scope she worked like a Trojan.

The menfolk, old Robert and Keith, had been to an agricultural sale, and Nanny had gone along for the ride. When the shooting brake returned she was the first out, and the first into the house, sniffing the aroma of baking. Of course Alison was a good cook, she had taught her herself. She smiled at her two girls, and tutted at Daisy, 'Eating biscuits? You'll spoil your appetite. Put that tin away!'

'Yes, Nanny,' said Daisy.

'I'll get out of my hat and coat and have a bit of a wash,' said Nanny, and went off to her room, which was still next to a room that had been the nursery and would never be again. Because when Alison and Keith's children came along it would be their mother who cared for them. They would sleep and play and live in the heart of the family.

Daisy and Alison laughed silently at each other. Nanny's bossiness was her way of caring, and she cared more for them than she did for herself. She made them smile when she ordered them about, but they never hurt her feelings if they could help it.

Daisy took out another biscuit, then shut the lid and replaced the tin on the dresser shelf, and said, 'I'm expecting a good meal, but it is a new place, I don't know what the food's like and I'd hate my tum to start rumbling.'

Daisy usually took her evening meal here unless she had a date. Tonight she had. She had been invited to dinner at a recently opened roadhouse and she should be getting along to her cottage and getting ready to be collected, but she lingered to say hello to Uncle Bob and Keith.

The men came in together and Alison went into Keith's arms, making, as Daisy always thought, a super pair. Their quick embrace—his hug, her lips brushing his cheek—was over in a moment, but said more plainly than words that they were right for each other.

'Had a good day?' asked Alison.

'So-so, how about you?' Keith included Daisy in that, and she said,

'The man came to take a picture of the picture.'

Robert Lingard had seated himself in the big wooden armchair he always used in this room. He was a big man, into his seventies now, but with clear blue eyes in a weather-beaten face, and a booming voice you could hear across any field. Something in Daisy's voice made him look closer at her and ask, 'What about it?' and she said slowly,

19

'I don't think he was sorry to get away.' She hesitated. 'I think he found the portrait—disturbing.'

Alison gasped, 'What do you mean? It didn't fall down on him, did it?' Alison was a practical girl, and so used to the portrait hanging there that she hardly saw it any more. It was like part of the wallpaper. How could a dingy old painting disturb anyone?

'No,' said Daisy, 'it didn't fall on him, but I think he was scared it might.'

Old Robert grunted. Keith grinned, 'If he was that nervous are his photographs going to come out?'

'He took several,' said Daisy. 'He kept going——' she sucked in and blew out, mimicking unease. 'I asked him if the light was wrong, if he wanted the painting moved, and he said no, the light was all right. All the same, he was nervous.'

'Oh, you and your dark Lingards!' Alison sounded like Nanny. 'I suppose you pointed that window out to him with all the grisly details?'

'Of course,' said Daisy.

'No wonder the poor man looked askance at the painting.' Alison was tolerant of Daisy's preoccupation with the seamier side of the family tree. The dark Lingards were as unreal to Alison as the Black Death, which had come to the parish in 1556 and taken one in three of the villagers. They were history, dust, gone for ever. But if Daisy wanted to write about them Alison could think of no reason why she shouldn't.

Robert Lingard had given Daisy the most encouragement. He didn't take her literary ambitions very seriously, but it pleased him to see her poring over the old papers, and he enjoyed smoking his pipe at night after a hard day's work and listening to what she had written.

She was a clever little lass, his Daisy. So was Alison, a rare and lovely girl and a wife in a million. Old Robert believed he had no favourite, but in his heart of hearts Daisy

20

was his darling.

Alison knew that, and didn't mind. She was first with Keith, and Daisy was her dear sister, and the pet and baby of the household.

'Who isn't having any dinner?' Keith inquired, seeing only four places set.

'Daisy's got a date,' said Alison.

'Same one as last week?' Keith asked.

'No,' said Daisy.

'Finished with him, have you?' asked Uncle Bob, and Daisy opened big blue eyes,

'Of course not. He's a friend. You don't finish with friends.'

'I should see him off,' said Uncle Bob. 'Never trust a man who mumbles,' and Daisy burst out laughing.

'You'd make any man mumble, asking him what he earns and what his prospects are!'

Uncle Bob often took it on himself to question Daisy's dates, as though he didn't think any of them were good enough for her. When she met someone she really cared about she would have to keep him from here, until he was warned and ready to face Uncle Bob. So far it hadn't mattered. There hadn't been anyone who was more than a friend, with whom she could envisage a deep man-and-woman relationship.

'This one's an accountant,' said Alison.

'We've got an accountant,' said Keith. 'It's a builder we want, another couple of tiles came off last week. How about finding us a good roof repairer, Daisy?'

'Or a washing machine mechanic,' Alison gurgled. She told Keith, 'The washing machine's packed up.'

Daisy left them, laughing, calling, 'See you tomorrow!' then she hurried out of the house and down the track towards the copse and the cottage, with the dogs at her heels, the terrier keeping close, the peke following.

She always liked opening the cottage door and stepping

into her own little kingdom. She hadn't changed much in here. The furniture was comfortable: chintz rose-patterned covers over a couple of deep armchairs and a settee; a low button-back fireside chair; an old dresser, a round table, and four lattice-backed chairs. The kitchen was small but adequate with a bathroom leading off it, and upstairs three bedrooms, built under the eaves.

Daisy was using one bedroom as a study. She had her desk in there, and her typewriter, and all the papers referring to Frederick, the Georgian dark Lingard. Nobody minded what she brought out of the house. Uncle Bob had suggested the miniature himself and that stood on her desk while she was writing about this particular gentleman—if gentleman was the word.

She hurried changing, getting ready for her date who was the brother of a girl who worked with her, and with a few minutes to spare before he was due to arrive to collect her sat on the sofa with her feet up.

Michael Langley seemed nice, his sister Anne was a nice girl, and Daisy was looking forward to her evening out, but she wasn't exactly breathless with anticipation. Not for the first time she wondered if she was going to end up as a spinster aunt, although there was lots of time yet.

There was a streak of reserve in Daisy. Casual sex was not for her. She made no song and dance about other people's way of life, but this was her way, and she was sensitive enough to handle her affairs so that no one's pride was too badly bruised. Sometimes she was jeered at as a prude by young men who expected every girl to fancy them, then she would smile sweetly and say, 'Nobody's perfect. Not even you.' It was more difficult if they asked her to marry them, but on the whole her boy-friends stayed her friends, even after they had decided that Daisy Penrose was a fetching but stubborn girl, and there was absolutely nothing they could do about it.

Woo, the terrier, jumped up from his nap on the sheepskin rug as she swung her feet off the sofa, getting under-foot as he often did. If she wasn't watching she could regularly rely on Woo to trip her up, and he nearly sent her sprawling now so that she glared at him as she side stepped. 'You are such a dimwit!' she said, and he wagged his tail, in full agreement with whatever she was saying.

The peke, sitting with paws hanging over the edge of the low fireside chair, yawned like one who has seen it all before. He got under nobody's feet, and he looked at Daisy with a near-human expression of shared exasperation as she stroked his silky head.

Then his ears lifted a fraction and he began a rumbling growl, taken up by the terrier in a bout of full-throated incessant barking and a rush for the door. The peke had heard a strange car coming up the track, and the terrier was giving the alarm. Woo enjoyed barking, most of the time he yapped for no obvious reason, but when Cooch clued him he knew that he was on to a sure thing.

He was making so much noise that Daisy didn't hear the car draw up, and hardly heard the knock on the door. Both dogs were by her when she opened the door on the chain, Woo barking, Cooch growling. She said, 'It's all right,' to the dogs, and 'Hello,' to the man outside, then closed the door and slipped the chain, while the peke waited and the terrier yapped on.

When Michael Langley stepped into the cottage he was enchanted by its old-world charm, just as he had been by Daisy's fresh-as-the-morning prettiness. The cute bouncy little dog was part of the picture, and when Daisy begged, 'Do be *quiet*, Woo!' which had no effect at all on the barking, Michael said,

'Nice little chap.'

Most of her dates petted Woo, who loved it and quietened for the time it took to roll over and get his stomach scratched, while Daisy put on her coat and picked up her handbag.

'I'm fond of dogs,' said Michael, looking at the peke, and Daisy said hastily,

'That one isn't fond of people.'

She locked the door behind them and Woo went on barking. 'I've been looking forward to this,' said Michael, and she could admit quite honestly, 'And so have I.'

It was a succeful first date, and Daisy had the satisfaction of knowing that her escort thought so too. They compared tastes on food and books and TV programmes and the way the world was going, their opinions dovetailing, which was reassuring and augured well.

Even to the amenable way Michael said goodnight at the door of the cottage instead of suggesting a final drink inside, although he knew she lived alone and most men might have taken advantage of that. They were going to the theatre next week, and the week after that Daisy thought she might suggest providing a meal herself, perhaps asking Anne, Michael's sister, and her fiancé to make up a foursome.

The dogs welcomed her home, each in his own way, and when she went upstairs she was singing happily to herself. The door of her study was open, as she had left it, and glancing in, at the desk and the miniature, took her mind back to the photographs Jack Brady had taken a few hours ago of the painting. She wondered how they would come out. Tomorrow she would slip into the newspaper office and inquire.

She closed the study door and went along the tiny landing into her bedroom. She wanted to go on thinking about Michael, but she had shattered her romantic, dreamy mood, and for the life of her she couldn't see hazel eyes for black, or Michael's frank open features for a dark visage and a crooked smile . . .

The photographs were not bad at all. Margaret had the one she had selected on her desk when Daisy turned up at lunchtime. It should reproduce quite well, Margaret thought. Some of the depth of the painting was inevitably lost in a black and white photograph, but side by side with the old sepia study it should prove that the dark Lingards came from the same mould.

'Do you want this?' she asked, handing over the still damp proof, and Daisy thanked her.

The *Post* was published on Fridays, and the Friday the article appeared lots of Daisy's friends rang up to tell her they'd read it and ask when the book was due. There hadn't been a dark Lingard for a hundred years, and the family was not illustrious enough to have been publicly chronicled, so this was the first most of the readers of the *Post* had heard of the family scandal. It was quite a nine-day wonder, and Daisy was a little celebrity for the best part of a week.

It was also the first that most of her friends and colleagues had heard about her writing a book, and she almost wished she hadn't mentioned that in the article, because she knew that from now on every so often someone would ask if she had finished it yet. Her leisurely indulgence had turned into a task, and something else was bothering her that was harder to explain. It was as though she was no longer in charge of her characters.

She sat at the window in her study, with the Georgian miniature and the newspaper reproductions on the desk in front of her, and wondered if she should drop the whole project. She was half way through what had to be a partly fictitious account of Frederick Lingard's pursuit of his heiress, but suddenly it all seemed too real and too close. She could feel the menace, like eyes on her, and she moved impulsively, opening a drawer and putting in the photographs, turning the miniature face downwards on the desk.

Then she looked over her shoulder, out of the window. He stood motionless on the track, looking up at her. Dark clothes, dark hair, the dark Lingard come again . . .

25

CHAPTER TWO

DAISY stared, too frozen to even blink. When she did close her eyes she would not have been surprised if he had vanished when she looked again and the whole thing had been imagination, a warning that she had the dark Lingards too much on her mind. But he was still down there, and solid enough to throw a shadow.

She backed from the window. She couldn't remember feeling like this since she was a child, and Alison and Keith had teased her, 'A dark Lingard's coming to get you.'

She began to walk down the stairs, her fingers clutching the handrail. She didn't want to go outside and meet him, although all that had happened was that there was a man out there, walking towards Oak House, who had stopped to look at her cottage. As there was no one in the farmhouse right now she had to ask him who he was and what he wanted. And perhaps she had imagined his resemblance to the paintings and the photographs.

In the living room she took off her large round spectacles with the amber frames, that she wore for driving, watching films and plays, and sometimes for working. Most of the time she didn't mind life being a little myopic, most people and most things look better with the harsher details softened. She didn't want to see this man too clearly and perhaps when she did look at him again she would know she had made a mistake.

The dogs moved with her, but she said, 'No, stay here,' and stepped out of the cottage, shutting the door quickly behind her. Behind the door Woo began to yap, of course, and she could hear Cooch growling. Cooch would sense that she was uneasy, and she didn't want him launching an unprovoked attack.

The man was still there, as though he had expected her to come down and was waiting for her. He was the right height, they were tall; and the right build, giving an impression of quick-moving strength, although he hardly moved. He had the hawklike face, the hard jaw, the thick straight dark hair. In the portraits the hair had been smooth and orderly. His fell over his eyes and he tossed it back impatiently, and she thought—they would all do that. She knew why he was here, but she said automatically, 'Can I help you?'

Instead of answering he asked, 'Who are you?'

'Miss Penrose.'

'Not Daisy, the authoress?'

'I'm Daisy Penrose.'

He was smiling now. She had never seen the crooked smile before, only read of it. It was a wicked smile, a flash of white teeth, voice and eyes bright and mocking. 'I don't believe it,' he said softly. 'I was sure Daisy Penrose would be a little old lady with silver hair.'

It was an old-fashioned name, it did sound like a little old lady, but there was no way in which she could have smiled back. The muscles of her face and throat were so rigid it almost hurt to speak. 'Who are you?' she said jerkily. 'What do you want?'

'I'm Richard Lingard.' Hugo the first, Roger, Frederick of the miniature, the Victorian Charles of the photograph, and now Richard.

Richard spoke with a slight American accent, that had to be a change, and there was no way of knowing if they had all had the same slow drawling voice.

She had never contemplated meeting a dark Lingard. He should have been extinct, and she was still staring at him in a daze when he said, 'Good morning, it's been a pleasure

27

to meet you, Miss Penrose,' as though he was going to continue his walk up to the house.

Then she got out, 'All the family have gone to church.'

Nanny and Uncle Bob always did, on Sunday mornings. Alison and Daisy and Keith less regularly. This morning only Daisy had defaulted, oversleeping, and had stayed behind, the only one here when the dark Lingard came home.

She shook her head, trying to shake sense back into her muddled mind, because whoever he was this was not his home.

The spire of the church rose in silhouette over the tree-tops and she looked towards it, willing him to go, telling him, 'They'll be coming out in ten minutes or so. You could walk round and meet them.'

'I wouldn't know them,' he explained, gently as though she was the village idiot. 'I'll walk up to the house and wait there.'

They should know him. They knew what the dark Lingards looked like, and of course they would find him if he waited until the service ended. Congregations were sparse enough these days. All he had to do was stand there, and the first person who came out would point out the Lingards to him. It was as though he were more interested in seeing the house than the family, and as he turned to walk up the wide track she said, 'I'll come with you.'

He raised an eyebrow, and she flinched as the eyes seemed to probe into her brain. She wasn't being helpful and he knew it. She was staying with him because she felt that she must keep an eye on him, as though he was a thief in the night although it was broad day.

The questions she should be asking were obvious. Where had he come from and exactly what kind of relation was he? But her tongue was sticking to the roof of her mouth and he took no further notice of her.

He walked with a long fast stride, unsmiling now, missing

nothing, she was sure. The artists had got the eyes right, they were piercing, and she was convinced that he would forget no single detail of what he saw.

Where *had* he come from? He had walked up the drive, no car. He was wearing dark slacks, a navy blue shirt with the top couple of buttons undone, and a dark blue and red kerchief knotted around his throat; he carried nothing. He hadn't come far, unless he had left his car in the road at the bottom of the track. Daisy tried to be calm, but she could still hardly believe her own eyes.

Now he was looking up at the house. saying nothing, his expression showing nothing. Then he began to walk around the side, towards the stable block and the back of the house, all the time noting, checking. Well, that was how it seemed, as though he was weighing the place up for some reason.

Standing by the stable block, Daisy found herself holding her breath, waiting to see if he would stare at the top end window a fraction longer. That showed how jittery she was, wondering if he knew what had happened in that room up there, and if there was such a thing as reincarnation and all the dark Lingards were really one man.

Pull yourself together before you go right out of your tiny mind, she chided herself. But when he went towards the back door that she knew was locked her instincts warned her against letting him into the house, and she wished she had the courage to deny him access. If she pretended she didn't have a key he would get in as soon as the family returned, but at least she wouldn't have let him in. And what difference would that make? And how could it matter?

At the door he turned to look at her. 'You want to go in?' she asked, feeling the words dragged out of her, and he smiled the crooked smile.

'Thank you,' he said, as though her offer had been a whole-hearted welcome.

29

There was nothing she could do but go for the spare key that was hidden in the stable block. She could have returned home for her own front door key to Oak House, and by then the family should have been back from church, but that might mean leaving him here alone, and she felt that he should be watched, guarded against. He was a threat on which she was unwilling to turn her back.

She came out quickly with the key, then walked slowly to put it into the keyhole and turn. She let him in first, and he went ahead of her down the passage. A tall man with broad shoulders, filling the narrow passage, and striding on with an arrogance that seemed out of place in a visitor and a stranger, even if he did carry the Lingard name.

He walked past the domestic quarters into the hall, and she said, 'In here, please,' and opened the study door. If she took him into that room she could watch out for the family, because it was at the front of the house. She could tap on the window and beckon and call them in, but he didn't seem to hear her.

He was examining the paintings on the panelled wall and she spoke loudly. 'Are you an artist?'

'No.'

'A dealer?' She made that query as pointed as she could, the way he was looking at the paintings he could have been pricing them, but he just said,

'A photographer.' As he moved away to climb up three stairs and inspect an etching she called sharply after him,

'As I don't really know who you are I don't think you should be wandering around in here.'

He began to laugh, as if that was funny. Then the laughter subsided into the crooked smile and he said with a courtliness that was pure mockery, 'They have an excellent watchdog in you, Miss Daisy Penrose. Would you allow me to see the painting of Hugo Lingard?'

The first dark Lingard. She indicated the dining room and said, 'In there,' and stood in the doorway, as he went in

30

and halted at his first sight of what could have been a portrait of himself painted centuries ago.

She heard his muttered ejaculation, 'Lord Almighty!'
and asked,

'Weren't you expecting him to look like you?'

'Not that much.' He walked across the room to stand in
front of the painting.

'Didn't you know you were a dark Lingard?' she persisted.

'So it's beginning to seem.'

'Just exactly who are you?' Now she had found her
voice her superstitious confusion had gone and she would
have questioned him, but they both heard the footsteps
that meant the family was back and she murmured, 'Excuse
me.'

Uncle Bob and Keith were crossing the hall Their surprise at seeing Daisy was because she was wide-eyed and
flushed. It would have been nothing unusual to have found
her in the house, she was expected for the rest of the day,
but she was obviously upset and both men were alarmed.

She sounded breathless. 'There's a man who says he's
Richard Lingard. He's in there.'

They went to the open door of the dining room. He still
stood under the painting, but facing the doorway now. He
smiled the crooked smile and they gasped, their faces
studies of astonishment.

'Who are you?' Robert Lingard's booming voice had
lost its resonance.

'Andrew Lingard——' the man began, and Robert said,
'Not Andrew's son?'

'His grandson, Richard.'

Uncle Bob had had two brothers. John had been Keith's
grandfather, Andrew had emigrated to America when he
was a young man and lost touch with everyone here, and
now Robert's gaze misted. If this caller was Andrew's flesh

31

and blood he was welcome. Robert held out a great hand and said, 'You're welcome.'

'Thank you, sir.' The answering grip was strong, the dark steady eyes met Robert's, who asked haltingly,

'Is my brother——?'

'He died before I was born.'

Robert Lingard had lost his two younger brothers many years ago. John had died, and he had given up hopes of ever seeing Andrew again. But sometimes he had wondered if a letter might still come, or an old man might knock on the door.

He had feared that Andrew was dead, but hearing it confirmed he sighed and shook his head and said, 'He was a fine young chap, the pick of the three of us,' and then more briskly, 'Well, there's no denying you're a Lingard,' chuckling at this unlikely situation. 'We thought we'd seen the last of them.' He looked at the man, then at the painting, and his smile widened, deepening the deep wrinkles. 'But most of it was old wives' tales, eh? And you can't help what you look like, can you, lad?'

Richard Lingard grinned too, taking a joke against himself. 'I reckon not,' he said, 'but it'll take some getting used to. I thought I was unique. I never thought there were photographs and pictures of me going back that far. I hope none of you folk believe in reincarnation.'

The men laughed heartily, but Daisy's lips tightened. She didn't actually believe he had lived before, but she did believe in genes, heredity traits, and someone who looked so like his ancestors was probably like them under the skin too. They had all been dangerous men, and she would have been happier if Keith and Uncle Bob had remembered that, instead of hailing Richard Lingard like the return of the prodigal.

Keith was saying, 'This is fantastic! Our fathers must have been cousins, so what relations are we? Second cousins?'

'Whatever we are,' said Richard, 'it looks as though you're my family.'

Daisy stood apart, watching Uncle Bob and Keith falling over themselves to make Richard Lingard feel at home. She had never seen Uncle Bob so chuffed. It took a great deal to stir him out of his phlegmatic attitude to almost everything, but now he was steering Richard Lingard into a sitting room, telling Keith to get out the whisky, telling Daisy to fetch Alison and Nanny.

Daisy went into the kitchen, where Nanny and Alison were checking on the joint they had left cooking, turning on the hotplates under saucepans of vegetables, and starting to lay the table.

'Hello,' said Alison as Daisy walked in, and Daisy said,

'I shouldn't bother laying that table, I think we'll be eating in the dining room. We've got a guest.'

Alison was pleased. 'Oh, who is it?' and Nanny, who considered it ill-mannered of guests to arrive without warning at mealtimes, was dubious.

'A relative,' said Daisy.

That puzzled them. 'Name of Richard Lingard,' she said. 'He claims he's Andrew's grandson.'

Nanny could remember Andrew, and she almost dropped the knives and forks she was placing. 'God bless my soul!' she quavered. 'Where is he?'

'In the small sitting room. Uncle Bob said to fetch you.'

Away went Nanny while Alison fumbled with her apron fastening, asking, 'What's he like?'

'Come and see,' said Daisy. She felt that she must be sounding unnatural. Her light tone and manner were so forced, she was filled with such apprehension, but Alison didn't seem to notice as she tossed her apron on to a chair and said cheerfully,

'This is exciting, isn't it? Nobody ever knew what happened to Andrew, did they? Is he nice?'

Daisy knew the answer to that—No, he is not—but she

33

could hardly say it, and Alison was off to see for herself.

Daisy went slower. When she reached them Nanny was giving little chirrups of delight, 'Oh, my goodness, I never did—oh, this *is* a surprise, oh, my!' The more Lingards the better so far as she was concerned. She was beaming at the newcomer with complete approval.

Alison had just been introduced, and was looking as pleased as Nanny and saying much the same about the unexpectedness of it all. But Daisy was more surprised than either of them, that they couldn't see he was Hugo and Charles and Frederick.

He wasn't standing under the painting now, so there was no immediate comparison. He had just got up from an armchair in the sitting room, a big man radiating warmth and charm and health and vitality. But surely they only had to look at the face, and imagine it still as the old portraits, to recognise it.

She tried to smile. 'He's a dark Lingard. Isn't that incredible? After a hundred years another dark Lingard!' She tried to keep her voice light, but it came out shrill enough to make them all look at her, and to shut up Nanny and Alison in mid-sentence.

'Sorry about that,' said Richard Lingard softly, 'but I guess there's not much I can do about it.'

Daisy heard what he said, but she felt he was telling her —there's not much *you* can do. They had all looked at her when she spoke, but his eyes stayed on her, and something flashed and crashed between them. There was no warmth in his eyes when he looked at Daisy.

Alison gurgled, 'So you are. What a lark! Did you know that?'

'Not until very recently.'

'Never mind,' said Alison gaily. 'They wouldn't be considered anything out of the ordinary in these permissive times, so we won't hold it against you,' and he clasped her hand in both of his, smiling his glittering smile, handsome

34

as the devil, playing up to Alison's teasing.

'Thank you, ma'am. That's a load off my mind. It's good to meet understanding folk, particularly when they turn out to be your own kin. And if I didn't look this way I wouldn't be here and I should have missed the great pleasure of meeting you all.'

It seemed he was in England on a working holiday, and he had picked up a newspaper with Daisy's article in. There was his name, his likeness to the two portraits, and then he had remembered hearing that his grandfather had originally come from this village.

Last night he had driven over, booked in at the pub and this morning followed the publican's directions to Oak House Farm.

After dinner, said Uncle Bob, he would go right back to the Three Feathers and bring his car and cases. He was staying here, for as long as he liked. There would be no problem finding him a room under this roof, as he could see for himself.

'That's very kind of you, sir.' Richard sounded genuinely appreciative, 'but I shouldn't care to cause anyone any trouble,' and both Nanny and Alison added their urging to Uncle Bob's, insisting that he would be no trouble, and that it was unthinkable that one of the family should be staying at the Three Feathers instead of here, in the family home.

He could have his grandfather's old room, said Uncle Bob, the only one who knew which that room was, and at that Richard accepted. Uncle Bob boomed, 'That's settled, then; this is going to be a day to remember,' and beamed with paternal pride on them all.

Only Daisy seemed to have any reservations. 'A day to remember' had a double meaning. They could recall the day Richard Lingard had arrived here with regret, rather than happy memories. Wasn't it called a gut reaction when your blood and every cell in your body was warning you?

And that was what she was getting, so strong a foreboding that she couldn't stay in the room. If she did she would begin to babble protests.

She moved quietly to the door, but he saw her, the dark eyes fixed her. 'You're not leaving us?' he asked, and she gulped,

'I'm going—to fetch my dogs.'

'To set them on me?' They all laughed, and again she felt completely detached from this scene of bonhomie.

'A West Highland terrier and a peke,' Keith elaborated, and Richard said,

'A peke, of course. Daisy Penrose should certainly have a pekingese.'

'Wait till you see this one,' Alison giggled, and Daisy left them.

They were all of them charmed by him, and that was entirely in character. Men stayed their friends and women loved them till the bitter end. In the olden days they had ridden rough-shod, taking what they wanted, and that man to whom Uncle Bob had just offered a home for as long as he wanted it was dangerous.

Because Daisy had spent so many hours getting together the data about the other dark Lingards she knew the signs. She would not have welcomed him if it had been left to her, but it was out of her hands now. He was here. And her fault. If she hadn't planned the book, and written the article, it was unlikely he would have remembered the name of the village where his grandfather was born, much less bothered to visit it. She had brought the dark Lingard here, as surely as though she had conjured him up with a black magic spell.

She turned back on the track to look again at the house. Unchanged for centuries, it had always had a golden warmth of security for Daisy, but today it seemed to be shadowed in the sunshine because of the intruder inside.

As she opened the door of her cottage the dogs came towards her. Woo dancing with excitement, Cooch catching the scent of her fear. She *was* frightened. Meeting that man had been traumatic. Daisy had always been the bookworm, the one for poring over the past. The rest of them didn't *know*, not even Uncle Bob, although she read most of her writing to him. A lot of her book was fiction, of course, but she had always tried to keep everything about the dark Lingards in character. She knew what they were capable of. She knew.

But if she said, 'He will harm us, they always did,' they would laugh at her. So would Richard Lingard, the way he had laughed in the hall when she had tried to stop him wandering off into the house.

No one really took Daisy seriously, not even her family. They loved her, spoiled and cherished her, but they would certainly dismiss her qualms about Richard Lingard as much ado about nothing. She and her dark Lingards had always been a family joke. Even Uncle Bob would say, 'Now then, Daisy-girl,' and Nanny would cluck as she had when Daisy was a child and going off into some childish flight of fancy.

Daisy pushed her soft curls from her aching forehead, for the first time up against the debit side of looking less astute than she was. I look like a dumb blonde, she thought bitterly, and nobody is going to listen to any warning I give them, not even Alison. Perhaps she should wear her spectacles all the time, they might make her look more intelligent.

Cooch stayed very close to her on the walk back to the house and she talked soothingly to him, assuring him that everything was fine. It was ironic that the only one on her wavelength should be a dog. He knew something was amiss and unless she calmed him he was capable of taking a piece out of Richard Lingard, which would result in Cooch being banished and Richard Lingard being even firmer established as an injured party. Woo would, of course, join the family group around him, all tail-wagging welcome.

In the kitchen Nanny was making the gravy, looking pleased as Punch, and Daisy wished that she could be sharing in the general joy. She had never been alone before, she had always felt as the family did, and a new relative from overseas should have been a cause for rejoicing. It would have been if he had looked differently; but he was what he was, and nobody but Daisy had any understanding of what that meant.

Nanny smiled at her. 'It's nice he's found his family,' she said.

'Doesn't he have a family in America?' Nanny was a brisk rather than sentimental soul, but now her voice was gentle and it was Daisy who sounded tart.

'No,' said Nanny, sighing over the gravy as she stirred. 'He isn't married, there's only him left.'

'Just him.' Daisy stood still, arms folded and held tight and stiff. 'No father, mother, brother, sisters? Just him?'

Nanny looked up as though Daisy was being childish and thoughtless, and said reprovingly, 'There's nothing unusual about folk being on their own, more's the pity.'

Daisy knew that. There was only Alison and Keith, and Uncle Bob and Nanny, in her family. But it was as though Richard Lingard had stepped out of a void. If he had had a background and some other relations it would have been less eerie. Perhaps 'eerie' was the wrong word, because whatever he was it was flesh and blood.

Daisy said, 'So he's found us. How long do you think he's going to stay here?'

Before Nanny could hazard a guess Alison whirled into the kitchen, bright-eyed, and still laughing at something one of the men must have said. She pounced on Daisy. 'Come *on*, we're having a marvellous time! He's a smashing bloke, he's been absolutely everywhere.'

'What happened to Andrew?' Daisy asked.

'What? Oh, he had a shop. He died a long time ago.'

38

'And his son?'

'Richard's father? He was a Richard too. He was in the navy, killed in the Philippines.' Alison had looked grave at that, now she smiled again. 'Don't start cross-questioning *me*, Richard will tell you all about it.'

'Dinner's ready,' said Nanny.

'Good,' said Alison, 'that was what I came in for. We'll get them into the dining room. Come on, Daisy.'

Richard was talking, Uncle Bob and Keith were listening and chuckling. When Daisy walked into the room Woo bounded ahead of her including everyone, even the stranger, in his friendly overtures. Cooch stood four-square, picked out Richard Lingard and silently bared his teeth. Richard Lingard said, 'I never saw a pekingese that size before.'

'He's a lion dog,' said Daisy. 'There aren't many of them.'

'I'm not surprised!'

'He's very anti-social,' Alison apologised. 'He tolerates us but he doesn't really care for anybody but Daisy. Woo's the friendly feller.'

Woo banged his tail and panted engagingly, and got himself patted by Richard, who looked at Cooch and said, 'Now I see why you feel safe enough, living alone in the cottage.'

'How do you know I live alone?' Daisy demanded hotly, and then blushed hotly because it was obvious they had told him so.

Alison said, 'Dinner's ready. This way, Richard.'

Uncle Bob took his usual seat, in the carver chair at the head of the table. Usually when they dined in the dining room Keith sat on one side of him and Alison on the other, but today Richard sat opposite Keith so that there were three Lingard men together, for the first time that Daisy could remember. Alison sat by Keith and Daisy found herself next to Richard.

It was better than facing him, but having him at the same table was enough to take away her appetite. There was no ignoring him. He had plenty to tell them, he did seem to have travelled everywhere, taking photographs he said which he sold to magazines and newspapers back in America. He was a good raconteur, he could paint word pictures and he had a host of anecdotes that kept everyone but Daisy laughing.

He was the cosmopolitan, they were the stay-at-homes, but he drew them all into the conversation, even Nanny. Everyone but Daisy. When he addressed her directly she answered so shortly that he grinned and afterwards left her alone.

She knew she was prejudiced. To the rest he was a man of immense charm and personality, revelling in the company of his new-found family. It was all spontaneous and natural and couldn't be going better. So Daisy was prejudiced, but it all seemed to her it was going too well, as though Richard Lingard was manipulating them and establishing himself.

Nanny was promising some real English cooking to show him what he had been missing all these years. Keith was suggesting he might come along to the races. They talked of local beauty spots he must see, and Uncle Bob reminisced about his grandfather's favourite fishing spot, a stretch of river that hadn't changed since Andrew Lingard caught a fifteen-pound pike there fifty years ago.

He's staying on, thought Daisy. He's accepted and he's staying, and Richard Lingard said, 'I certainly do like this country. Even before I knew I'd got an English family I was thinking of making a permanent home here.'

'You could do a lot worse,' said Uncle Bob, and Alison and Keith and Nanny all chorused agreement. Daisy asked quietly,

'Don't you have a home?'

'I take apartments where I need them. Maybe it's time I put down roots and started looking for a house to buy.'

'The Lingard roots are here all right.' Alison was thinking how nice it would be for Keith to have another man in the family, then she saw Daisy's downcast eyes and the disapproving droop of her sister's lips and smiled mischievously and suggested, 'You could always help Daisy finish her book. To bring it right up to date she ought to be making a study of you.'

Daisy's eyes had widened in a furious glare at Alison, who went on smiling.

'So she should,' drawled Richard Lingard. His sidewards glance held nothing but amusement at Daisy's discomfiture, but his body, near her but not touching her, had tensed. She sensed, rather than saw, an involuntary withdrawal and wondered if it was natural reserve—who would want someone who seemed to dislike them asking personal questions? —or if he really had something to hide. Whatever it was he need not worry. She was getting no closer to him than she had to. He could keep his secrets.

'Nobody knows more about the history of the Lingards than Daisy does,' Alison persisted, and Richard said,

'I'd be interested to hear it.'

'Then Daisy's your girl.'

Daisy looked daggers at Alison. She couldn't be at her matchmaking with *this* man—but Alison smiled blandly back. They were all smiling, and Daisy recognised the old familiar loving teasing. Now they expected her to smile too, coaxed out of her silence to make a flippant retort that was perhaps even a little flirtatious. Richard Lingard was an attractive man, and Daisy was a honey-child, and the two were bound to get on famously. That was what they thought. But she felt older and colder than she had ever felt in her life.

Uncle Bob said benevolently, 'Daisy's the one to show you round.'

'I'd appreciate that.' He sounded as he had done when she'd asked if he wanted to go into the house, as though she was being most hospitable. She couldn't say, 'You're

41

welcome,' and she could hardly say, 'I will not.' She said coolly,

'Of course.'

It was true that she knew more about the house and the family than anyone else. She would pretend that she was showing a stranger around. He was a stranger, and she didn't speak to him again.

When the meal was over she helped Nanny and Alison clear the table, and turned on Alison as soon as they reached the kitchen demanding furiously, 'Why did you have to do that? I don't want to show him round. I don't want anything to do with him!'

Alison took her place at the sink, stacking the plates for washing. 'Go on,' she said cheerfully, 'you know you've always been waiting for a dark Lingard.'

'*No*,' Daisy protested.

Nanny bustled her out of the way. 'He's a nice young man,' said Nanny. 'Respectful too. You don't see much respect for their elders these days.'

Daisy had noticed the ease with which he adapted, how surely he had summed them up and got them on his side. All the dark Lingards had been loaded with calculating charm.

Keith looked round the kitchen door to say, 'Daisy, you're wanted. He really is interested in the old times. He wants to hear all about them.'

'I'm washing up,' said Daisy, and Nanny jerked the tea towel out of her fingers.

'Now you stop being silly,' scolded Nanny as though Daisy was ten years old, 'and go and talk to him.'

Uncle Bob and Richard Lingard were still in the dining room. Both stood up as Daisy walked reluctantly into the room, and Uncle Bob said, 'Now Daisy will be able to tell you everything. She's writing a book about the family.' He knew that. He'd seen the article about the book. 'She's a librarian,' said Uncle Bob fondly, 'and she's a very clever girl.'

She had never minded before being treated like a promising child, but she resented Richard Lingard's sardonic expression, and said crisply, 'I've been writing it since I was nineteen, and that's three years ago. What can I tell you? What do you want to know?'

Uncle Bob went out of the room. She would rather he had stayed, but he usually took a nap after his midday meal on Sundays, and he was probably getting it in while Daisy took the newcomer round Oak House.

'Where did you get the material for this book?' asked Richard Lingard.

'From the family papers. I've been working on them for a long time, getting them into some sort of order. Most of those about the dark Lingards are down in my cottage. I'll bring them up here and you can read them if you like.' That presumed he would be staying long enough to read them, and he didn't deny it. It also made it clear that she wasn't inviting him into her home.

'Thank you,' he said. Daisy stood with her arms folded tightly. He stood relaxed, looking up at the oil painting, asking, 'Old Hugo there was the original?'

'The first dark Lingard? Yes, although I suppose the dark stranger was the original.'

This was in the article, and he smiled the crooked smile, 'Pirate or devil?'

'That's what they said.'

'Rather inland, isn't it, for a pirate?' He was disbelieving and amused. 'Or was he supposed to have sailed up the river flying the skull and crossbones?'

'Of course not.' She didn't care if she seemed to have no sense of humour, because right now she hadn't. Her voice was fast and flat. 'He came to live in a house near here. There's no mention exactly where it was, but it was a big house and he was rich and nobody knew where his money

43

had come from, and that was what people said at the time, that he was a pirate or the devil.'

'What happened to him?'

'He sailed off.'

'A welsher as well as a pirate?'

She seized on that. 'The rest took after him. None of them was strong on responsibility.'

It was a strange sensation, standing here talking to a dark Lingard. Not putting words into their mouths as she had done for her book, not knowing what the words were going to be. He drawled,' 'They must have felt some responsibility to this place if the "black streak" is in the direct line of inheritance. Weren't they all, in their time, master around here?'

'Yes. Every one of them. Oh, they kept the house and the farm going all right,' she said scornfully. 'They made the money. Materially they did jolly well, and they didn't care how. Hugo probably started with the murder of his brother to get the place. Then there was abduction, rape, blackmail, gambling, of course, and possibly a little simple thieving.'

She hadn't expected to shock him. She wasn't surprised when he laughed and said, 'They sound a bunch of hard-working guys.'

'Hard-living!' she cried. 'Selfish, cruel!' Her denunciation rang out and his query was reasonable.

'If you feel that way why are you going to the trouble of documenting them?'

Oh, how Daisy wished now that she had left them alone. She was embarrassed by her over-emotional outburst and she tried to explain. 'It was just a hobby. Something to write about that had happened here a long time ago. I never thought——'

'You never thought you'd meet a devil that was breathing?'

She saw the slow rise and fall of the dark hairs on the

44

chest beneath the open-necked shirt. She was breathing shallowly, her clasped hands trembling a little.

'You can stop shaking,' he said, 'because you still haven't.' He shrugged powerful shoulders. 'O.K., I look like Hugo there, but I've never pushed anybody out of a window.' He grinned. 'And I haven't abducted any heiresses lately, it's harder to make a fortune these days.'

She nearly smiled. 'And I'll wager,' he went on, 'that every time a boy was born in this family with black hair and this kind of face he was a marked man. Everybody would be waiting for that devil's streak to break out.'

'Well, it did,' she retorted, 'in all of them.'

'What were the rest?' he jeered. 'Plaster saints?'

'I don't suppose so, for a minute. They were—ordinary.'

'Allowances are made for ordinary men. And no one's done a hatchet job on their memory.'

'You could be right,' she said silkily. Then she added, 'But you're not. Do you want to see round and hear a few dates and details?'

He made a half bow. 'Lead on, Miss Daisy.'

Miss Daisy! Big blue eyes and golden curls, but she would not be playing her sweet and simple role for this man. She said, 'Would you mind if I called you Dark Richard?' and he made a grimace of distaste.

'I most certainly would. It sounds like an after-shave.'

'And Miss Daisy sounds like lavender water, so it's either Miss Penrose or Daisy. I don't care which.'

He was laughing, but she felt she had scored. As she stepped ahead of him Cooch moved too, getting between her and Richard, and she said, 'You don't need to worry about Cooch. He won't bite unless he thinks you're attacking me.'

'Thanks for the warning, I'll remember that,' said Richard.

Woo trotted forward too, right under her feet as she looked over her shoulder, and she lurched, grabbing for the table's edge, missing it and landing in ungainly fashion on her knees. Richard Lingard could have caught and steadied her, but he stood grinning.

As she got up he said, 'Does Cooch know the difference between an attack and a helping hand? I thought he might have been listening to your talk on rape.'

'I was not talking about rape, I just listed it.' She had bruised her knee and her dignity, and she would have liked to yell at him. Or at Woo, who had scuttled away as he always did after he had tripped her up.

Now the dog's bright eyes watched in supplication from a corner while Daisy demanded as always, 'Why do you *do* it?'

'Is this a regular thing?' asked Richard.

'He will get underfoot.'

'One dog homicidal and the other manic? You keep peculiar pets!'

'Cooch is sometimes a little anti-social, that's all, and Woo is not mad, he's thick. Now, do you want to hear the family history?'

'That is why they've left us alone, isn't it?' He was deliberately trying to disconcert her, amused at her disapproval of him, and she said tartly,

'One of the reasons they're all keeping out of the way is because, now you've turned up, they want me to forget about the dark Lingards. They think if we have to talk to each other we're bound to make friends.'

She hadn't meant to say this, but it was why she had been manoeuvred into this predicament. Having said it she waited, looking at the face she knew so well. The living face and the painting on the wall both communicated a danger that had made poor Jack Brady cringe.

'And do you suppose we are going to be friends?' asked Richard Lingard. Daisy answered, huskily and honestly,

'I think it unlikely.'

The eyes were not black, as the reports and the paintings

46

made them. They were very dark grey. She saw that now. He began to smile, but still there was no warmth in his eyes. 'I agree,' he said. 'Most unlikely.'

CHAPTER THREE

DAISY had never reeled off the family history for anyone before, and she was surprising herself at how much she knew. As they walked through the house Richard Lingard listened attentively. He didn't ask many questions, but he looked around him with that swift searching glance so that Daisy asked, 'Looking for anything in particular?' and he said gravely,

'Admiring the decor.'

'Alison will be pleased,' said Daisy, with the slightest edge of sarcasm. 'She does all the decorating. Nanny helps, and so do Keith and I, but we're out during the day so we don't have much time.'

He seemed surprised. 'Why doesn't she get the professionals in?'

'Because professionals want paying.' She wondered if he had thought the family wealthy, and added, 'There's no money for decorators. It's all Uncle Bob and Keith can do to keep solvent,' and she saw, briefly, a hooded look like a mask on his face, hiding—could it be disappointment? Gone in a flash, the smile back again.

'Keith should have followed Frederick's example and looked around for an heiress,' he said.

That was pretty insulting to Alison, but Daisy wasn't losing her temper. 'Not being a dark Lingard Keith chose to marry for love,' she said sweetly.

'How do you know Fred wasn't in love with his moneyed mistress?'

She was supposed to be telling him the family history, so

she put him right on that. 'The poor girl wasn't his mistress while she had any choice. She was bundled into a carriage while she was out walking. For a month or so her friends and relations searched high and low, and then she turned up married to Frederick.'

'That must have been quite a month.'

She didn't look at him. If she had done she had a crazy feeling that she might have blushed. She walked on down the passage, and he asked as though it was a serious query, although he was obviously laughing at her, 'And how are you handling this delicate situation in your book?'

Daisy hadn't reached the missing weeks yet, she was still leading up to the kidnapping. She snapped, 'Well, I'm certainly not suggesting she liked him any better at the end of her ordeal than she did before, but if a girl went missing for one night in those days, let alone four weeks, there wasn't much she could do but get married as quickly as possible.'

'You don't think she might have known the carriage was coming?'

'It wasn't an elopement, it was an abduction.' That was enough about Frederick, she felt, and she said, 'The room at the end is the murder room.'

'Which murder?'

'How many do you want? This isn't the Tower of London. The window that Hugo pushed his brother from.' There was no real proof of that and in her book Daisy had left it an open question, but with Richard Lingard beside her she was prepared to portray all dark Lingards as villainously as possible.

The room was a store room, only containing cupboards and a large chest of drawers, but even now Daisy could recall her childhood horror of the place. She had been in her teens before she had ever stood by that window, and subconsciously there was still a hint of bravado as she flung open the door and stepped inside.

'From there,' she said, indicating the window. There were three horizontal bars across the lower portion, the window in this room was only about a foot up from the floor, and Richard Lingard pointed out,

'If the bars weren't there in Hugo's day, of course, his brother could have fallen through. After a couple of tankards of whatever they drank in those days.'

She said drily, 'You are trying to whitewash them, aren't you?'

'Wouldn't you in my place? It was bad enough seeing the newspaper reproductions, but the painting really shook me. I'll feel better if I can convince somebody that the dark Lingards might have been sinned against as well as sinning.'

If she hadn't known what she did about them he would have made her laugh. She would have warmed to the crooked smile and the gleam of mockery in the eyes. She said, 'I'm sure you'll convince them all.'

'Them?' An eyebrow raised. 'But not you?'

'Sorry, but I keep remembering how wily the dark Lingards always were. I'm sure they could have talked their way out of anything.'

A smile was tugging her lips in spite of herself, and when he made an exaggerated gesture of despair, exclaiming, 'I can't win!' she did laugh.

'And I'm sure you don't say that often,' she said.

'I'll have to watch you, you're a dangerous woman.' She couldn't tell if he was still joking. Whether he was or not she was certainly watching him as a dangerous man. He went to the window, looking out, and after a while he said, 'You'd be safe, even if the bars weren't on the window.'

Hanging back called for an explanation. Daisy moved to his side and said, 'I was scared stiff of this room when I was a child. It was like Bluebeard's chamber. Even now I'm not too happy about standing at the window.'

He didn't smile at that, although she had spoken lightly. He asked, 'You were here as a child?'

'I was born in the cottage. My family have lived here for generations, they worked on the farm. I come from a long line of hedgers and ditchers.'

'I'd have thought you came from a long line of milk-maids.' That was blatant flattery of her dewy complexion, and she received it like all the easy admiration that had come her way, with a smile. But, as she looked at him through the long lashes she had instinctively lowered, she felt his gaze on her like the brush of fingers on her cheek, feathering to her mouth and edging the full soft curve of her lips.

It was a physical sensation, so realistic that she almost believed he must have reached out and touched her. He hadn't, but she drew back a little and began to talk about the farm, how many men had worked here when she was a child and how the last two decades had decimated their numbers. She was into crop rotation when he asked, 'Are both your parents dead?'

'Yes.' He was waiting and she went on, 'I don't remember my mother, but Nanny was like a mother to Alison and me, and Uncle Bob was always Uncle Bob.' He still waited, but she didn't want to talk about herself, she almost felt she had said too much already. 'You must have been very young when your father died,' she ventured.

He said 'Yes,' and without giving her chance to get in another question, 'This has all been very interesting—and now I'd better see about collecting my car and cancelling my booking. Thank you for showing me round the house, I'm sure your book will be a great success.'

They were out of the room and into the passage, and Daisy had told him a little about herself, but he was offering no confidences in return. Not a thing.

They came to a bedroom door that had been closed when they passed it a few minutes ago. Now the door was open,

51

and Nanny and Alison were inside. 'What goes on?' Daisy asked, and Alison, who was standing with hands on hips, replied, 'We were wondering how to start in here.'

It was a small bedroom, still fully furnished but not used for a long time. The wallpaper was faded and the furniture was dulling, unpolished. Alison hadn't reached this room in her home decorating campaign yet, and Daisy wanted to know, 'Why do anything?' There was more than enough to cope with in the areas of the house still in general use, but Nanny explained,

'It was Mr Andrew's room.' And now offered to Richard. 'We'll soon get some bedding up,' said Nanny, eyeing the bare spring base of the bed.

'But it will still look pretty bleak,' said Alison, and apologetically to Richard, 'If you'd said you were coming we'd have got it ready for you.'

'Then I'm glad I didn't,' he replied. 'I've caused enough trouble, and the room's just fine.'

Nanny didn't agree. 'It needs a good clear out. It hasn't been used since I don't know when.' She was about to get down on her knees to examine the carpet closer, but Richard caught her arm.

'Oh no,' he said, 'I'm not having this—I'll stay on at the pub.'

'We have a guest room that only needs sheets on the bed,' said Alison, 'but don't you want your grandfather's room?' and Richard laughed.

'Under the family roof what difference is one room from another?'

'Good,' said Alison, relieved. 'That will make things easier,' and Daisy remembered the room she had just left and thought how different the atmosphere in there was compared with—say—the kitchen.

'It's all in the mind,' said Richard. He must have guessed her thoughts, she had looked thoughtful and half glanced back at the doorway, but she didn't want him guessing what she was thinking. 'I'm just going to fetch my car,' he said. 'I'll see you all in about half an hour.'

When he had gone Alison asked, 'Why didn't you go with him?'

'Why should I?' said Daisy. 'I've just given him a guided tour of the house, I've done my share of entertaining.'

Richard was back in just under half an hour when a grey Jaguar XJ6 drove into the courtyard, and Keith went out to show him where to garage it and to help carry in his baggage. He had a leather-strapped holdall, and one other case with his cameras in. He travelled light, but with a car like that he was obviously prospering.

Uncle Bob was up and about again from his nap by now and they all gathered in the small sitting room, the familiar family group making a different pattern today because another chair was drawn up and Richard Lingard had somehow shifted the central point.

Until today when the family was alone Uncle Bob, with his great girth and his booming voice, and the fact that he was head of the family, had been the solid one, the unmoving one. Today Richard was sitting on the other side of the hearth, facing Uncle Bob, and to Daisy at least he seemed the stronger. Physically of course he was stronger, he was forty years younger, but the way he sat, relaxed, controlled, with that aura of power, brought back his words to her, 'Weren't they all in their day master around here?'

Uncle Bob was master now, and after him Keith. But Keith was sitting in the background. Beside Richard, in the same kind of chair, but as overshadowed as though he was in another room.

No one else seemed to notice, and you always let a visitor take the spotlight. But it wasn't as though Richard was talking that much, Keith was saying more, and Uncle Bob—by no means a chatty man normally—was still reminiscing about his brother Andrew. Most of the time Richard listened, and Daisy watched and wondered that they couldn't see how completely he was at home, as though he had taken over.

She asked, during a lull in the talk, 'How long will you be staying?' and Uncle Bob remonstrated,

'The lad's only just come!'

'A day or two, if that's all right.' Richard looked at Uncle Bob, who told him,

'You've a home here for as long as you like.'

'Thank you,' said Richard.

'Don't you need to tell anyone where you are?' asked Daisy. 'Make a phone call?'

'No.' He looked at her now. 'I'm a free agent.'

'A photographer. What kind of photographs?' This was almost the first time she had spoken in fifteen minutes, which was unlike Daisy, and now she was sounding blunt as an interrogator.

'The English countryside at the moment,' he said. 'I might get some good shots around here.'

She wondered if his photographs would tell anything about him, the camera lens equating the human eye. How would he see this house? How did he see them? 'Places, not people?' she said.

'Anything that interests me.' The crooked smile flickered. 'I must take a photograph of you. Your hair and skin would make a first-class study in texture.' Again she felt his touch, fingers through her hair, her face cupped in his hands, and again she moved away, pressing her back against the back of her chair. Without changing the subject too abruptly she tried to steer it into another channel.

'The last press photographer who came here was taking the picture for the article about the dark Lingards. I suppose you're what they call a follow-up story. I must tell Margaret tomorrow.'

'Who's Margaret?' he spoke very softly.

'Margaret Cookson, the features editor of our local paper.'

The smile was replaced by the hooded look, although the voice was still soft. 'Sorry, but I've no intention of being featured as a freak. If you've any ideas of introducing me to anyone as a dark Lingard—much less to your local press— I'll be leaving now.'

Daisy should have been abashed by her brashness, everyone else was, but all the apology she could muster was a small grimace, even though Alison was hissing, 'For goodness' *sake*!' and Uncle Bob was shaking his head, disappointed at her.

'Another reason,' said Richard—and she said, 'Ah!' because she had known there was another reason—'I can do without too many questions into my background.'

'Are you a crook?' She *was* ashamed of that, that was a silly thing to say, and he answered tight-lipped,

'No, I'm a bastard.' Then with swift and savage courtesy, 'I apologise for the bluntness of that announcement. I'll put it this way. In keeping with the tradition of the first dark Lingard I am illegitimate. My father was killed in the Philippines before he could marry my mother. As you mentioned earlier,' he was looking straight at Daisy, telling her this, all his anger directed at her, 'I was very young at the time. Two months from conception, if you feel you're entitled to details, and as they had planned to marry on his next leave that makes me a bastard.' In the silence he said, 'A description that I'm sure will have your full endorsement.'

Hot colour scalded her face and he said cynically, 'I'm sorry I've shocked you.'

'Of course I'm not shocked.' Her voice caught in her throat. 'I'm—sorry, I'm just very sorry.' A man like him would have come to terms with the circumstances of his birth years ago, but to be forced to state them, to people he had met for the first time only hours before, was an intolerable invasion of privacy.

He looked away from her then at the others in a slow

55

sweeping glance that took in every face. If he was assessing their reaction it was uniform, heartfelt sympathy. Robert Lingard spoke for them all. 'That was hard on your mother.'

'Very,' said Richard, 'but it could have been worse; she had good parents.' He smiled wryly at Alison. 'Times were less permissive then and she passed herself off as a widow, for the benefit of the neighbours.'

'She was a widow,' said Robert emphatically. 'The wife of Andrew's son as surely as you're his grandson.'

'That was how we saw it,' said Richard. There wasn't much else that could be said, and an awkward moment stretched while everyone smiled encouragingly at him to make up for Daisy's gaffe. Then he stood up and announced, 'I'd like to take some photographs of you all. It isn't every day a man comes across a family group that turns out to be his own.'

'Right now?' Alison squealed.

'What better time?' said Richard.

It broke the tension. He fixed lights and took numberless shots. Nanny was protesting that she made a horrible photograph, all the time thrilled that Richard had recognised her as family. Alison fooled a little, pretending to be a model girl, making them laugh as Richard snapped professionally away. He took what might be super character studies of Uncle Bob and Keith, and Daisy posed meekly where he put her.

Everybody was happy again. The cosy atmosphere was back, and Daisy guessed that Alison was clowning to make up for her own silence. Daisy's spirits were at such low ebb that she couldn't have joked, it was all she could do to smile to order. She was still ashamed at having caused that sad little scene they had just gone through, and although everyone was enjoying themselves now, she was not.

She knew that Richard Lingard was a photographer taking photographs, but she could see a dark Lingard manipulating everybody in this room, telling them where to sit, how to look.

He directed her to a window and she went, standing in profile, lifting her head obedient to his command. But when he came across and took her chin in his hand, moving her head a further fraction, she stiffened, and he grinned and said softly, 'You don't believe the primitive myth that a photograph can take your soul away?'

'That's the first I've heard of that,' she said, through curved lips that were faking a smile.

'I thought you were the girl who knew all the old legends, and believed every one.'

'Then you're wrong,' said Daisy. 'I'm the girl who doesn't believe half she hears.'

She had hit, without even taking aim. What she had said was a reflex repartee, but a muscle moved in his cheek and she was suddenly suspicious that somehow he had lied to them.

He stood back, holding the camera so that it shielded his face, taking pictures of her from several angles.

He even photographed the dogs, posing Woo but having more sense than to try pushing Cooch around. Cooch sat, with dignity and slitted eyes, and when the photographic session was over and an evening with Richard Lingard loomed ahead Daisy said, 'I'll have to be leaving you—I'm going out this evening.'

This was the first the family had heard of a date and Alison demanded, 'Who with?'

'Oh, Michael,' said Daisy.

'I'll walk to the cottage with you,' said Alison, and as soon as they were outside the house, 'You only said that to get away, didn't you? You really do dislike him.'

'He makes me feel uncomfortable,' Daisy muttered.

'It's your own fault. Why do you keep on needling him?'

Daisy scuffed a stone from the path and offered, 'I'll keep out of his way,' and Alison laughed,

'The way you're going on it might not be a bad idea, just for a day or two.'

'For a day or two?' Daisy echoed.

'While he's here.'

'You think that will only be for a day or two?'

Alison had heard Uncle Bob offer the newcomer a home for as long as he wanted it. She had heard Richard talk about buying a house and settling in England. It was always possible his visit would be extended, and apart from Daisy's attitude Alison could see no objections. Oak House was big enough; cooking for one more wouldn't daunt her and Nanny.

She pointed out, 'He can't stay put too long, his job must keep him on the move even if he does buy a house round here.'

'*If* he buys a house,' said Daisy. They were coming to her own little cottage. 'If he doesn't settle for Oak House.'

'What are you talking about?' Alison was trying to follow this obscure line of thought which was so glaringly obvious to Daisy.

'Coming in?' said Daisy, on her doorstep, and when Alison shook her head, 'He's exactly the same relation to Uncle Bob as Keith is. He might decide he's got as much right to the place as Keith has.'

Alison trilled with merry laughter. 'I suppose it comes from working in a library, although you always did have a vivid imagination, you and your dark Lingards. Look, love,' she was trying to sound serious, with dancing eyes and lips quivering with mirth, 'Richard's no farmer, he wouldn't take our kind of life as a gift, and Uncle Bob would never do a thing like that to Keith. If it hadn't been for Keith where would the farm be? Uncle Bob knows that.'

'I hope so,' said Daisy. Alison went, still smiling, secure in her little world, convinced that her sister was the dreamer. But it was Daisy who had seen with clearer vision how Richard Lingard surpassed Keith. Richard was stronger than Keith, stronger than Uncle Bob. Strong enough, perhaps, to take from here anything he wanted.

One thing was sure—she would write no more about the dark Lingards. She would gather the old papers and her manuscripts together, put them in a box and get them into the attic of Oak House, where she would leave them and try to forget them. The fantasy was over and she would be glad when today was over.

A night's sleep must steady her. She made a cup of tea and tried to read, curled up on the sofa, the two dogs close by her. Woo was content, but Cooch was as tense as Daisy was, following each movement of her hands as she turned the pages, meeting her eyes with disconcerting intelligence whenever she looked his way.

After a while she put down her book, she couldn't concentrate on it, and decided to wash her hair and have a hot bath, both relaxing exercises. Then an early night, and hope she had no nightmares about dark Lingards.

Up at the big house they would be drawing the curtains as the shadows were falling, a close and loving family in the warm glow of lamplight. But tonight Richard was gathered in with them, and as Daisy drew her own red and white check gingham curtains she could almost believe she heard the laughter and the voices.

She didn't. It would have to be a really hilarious party for sound to carry this far. But she could imagine the scene, and she knew there would be laughter, and none of them would see that he was stagemanaging all this cheer. He was such good company, as well as being a relation, that they would all want him to stay just as long as he could.

After her bath she curled up on the sofa again, blow-drying her tumbled hair. Then, leaning her head against a cushion, she fell asleep. The dogs woke her out of a cramped slumber so that she winced with a stiff neck when she raised her head, and rolled off the settee grimacing and stretching.

Both were giving an alarm that meant someone was near

the cottage. Daisy had a chain on her door, so it should be safe enough to peer out, but when she saw by the clock on the wall that it was nearly nine she stayed where she was. Visitors were unlikely so late and, if it was family, Cooch who recognised footsteps even on turf would be wagging his tail by now instead of growling with fur on edge.

She took a couple of steps at the rat-tat of the door knocker, but when her name was called, and she knew who was out there, she froze again. Whatever had brought Richard Lingard along at this hour she didn't want to know, and she hoped that if she kept quiet he would think she was still out on her date and that she left on lights as a security precaution.

The curtains were drawn, and if he peered through the letter box he would only get a narrow view that didn't include Daisy. She clutched the long full skirt of her dressing gown against her, ducking down and away from the door. Then she saw the inch-wide gap in the curtains, and knew he only had to take a couple of strides from the door to get a full view of her in this ridiculous position.

She had no doubt he would look through the window, if he hadn't done so already before he knocked on the door, so she called, 'I'm coming!' hoping her voice conveyed nothing but irritation at being disturbed.

She said, 'Shut up, Woo!' and to Cooch, 'It's all right, I think,' then she opened the door on the chain just wide enough for her to look out, and for Cooch to present one glaring eye.

'Oh!' she said, as though she hadn't realised it until now. 'It's you—what do you want?'

She was sounding so ungracious that she could hardly have blamed him if he had snapped back, 'Not you,' but he said quite civilly, 'Your spectacles.' He was holding her spectacle case. She was always leaving her glasses behind at Oak House and having to dash up in the morning before she could drive herself to work.

She said, 'Thank you, but you needn't have bothered.'

'No trouble. I offered to bring them down and drop them through the letter box.'

'Then why didn't you?' He still wasn't handing them over. He was standing in the dark outside and a cold little wind was blowing into the room.

'Because I was curious about that date of yours.'

Daisy blinked. 'Why should my dates concern you?'

'He wouldn't be——' In the cottage, he meant, and before she could say, 'Of course not,' Richard said, 'No, of course not.' But she felt he was basing that on her appearance, which was hardly seductive. Her faded old blue flannel was fine when you were lolling about on your own, but it was hardly a hostess gown.

'It was an excuse, wasn't it?' said Richard. 'You walked out this evening because I was there.'

She could have been polite and denied it, but he knew that she had stayed in her cottage and alone. So she said, 'Yes.'

'This dark Lingard mumbo-jumbo?'

And other things. Although if he hadn't looked like the dark Lingards she wouldn't have been suspicious of him. She admitted, 'A lot of it probably is mumbo-jumbo and I'm probably prejudiced, but you agreed yourself it was unlikely we should ever be friends.'

The white teeth gleamed. 'With a built-in antipathy like yours it could be one hell of a struggle. May I come in, or would the neighbours talk?'

The only neighbours were wild life, the only watchers the night hunters and the owls. If she closed the door in his face she would be acting like a ninny, and if she continued to stand here in the draught she would be catching a cold. She stooped to Cooch. 'It's all right,' she said. But when she'd closed the door to slip the chain she decided it might be safer to put the peke into another room, and she called, 'Won't be a minute, I'm getting Cooch out of the way.'

61

The dog went unwillingly, but Daisy shooed him up the stairs and bundled him into her bedroom and shut the door on him. Then she came down and let in Richard Lingard, saying as she did, 'It's late for calling.'

'You keep early hours.'

'Any hour's late when I've had my bath and I'm ready for bed.' If she had been less nervous she would have worded that differently, and she was glad he didn't grin because she was not trying to be funny or provocative. But he looked quite serious, asking,

'May I sit down?'

'Of course.'

'Thank you.' He put the spectacle case on the table and took a chair, and as Daisy sat down again he said, 'It's meant a lot to me, finding a family like this. I don't want to upset anyone here.'

He didn't give the impression of being a lonely man. To Daisy he seemed quite self-sufficient, with no scrap of sentimentality. But perhaps all human beings need to belong, and finding you have a family when you had believed you were the last of your line must be tremendously exciting.

Uncle Bob was happy today, with the grandson of his brother, and Nanny and Alison and Keith had welcomed Richard with open arms. Daisy said, 'They're all delighted you've come.'

'Them. Not you,' he said as he had said before, emphasising again that she was the only sour note in this reunion. The crooked smile could be pleading as well as mocking, and when the dark hair flopped over the dark grey eyes it was an undeniably attractive face. 'All I'm asking,' he said quietly, 'is give me a break. Take me as you find me.'

She couldn't see why her approval mattered, except that Uncle Bob was fond of her and might be influenced a little by her sustained aversion to anyone. It would be hard for her to blot out a lifetime's obsession with the dark Lingards, and she gave the only assurance she could. 'I'll try.'

'That's good enough.' From overhead came what sounded like the booming of a great gong and Richard looked up at the ceiling, startled. 'What the blazes is that?'

'My pekingese,' said Daisy demurely.

'Would you care to explain what he's doing?'

'He sits up, begging you know, and bashes the door with his front paws. And they're old doors, warped, they don't fit snugly, so they bang.'

The booming noise went on. 'Sounds like King Kong,' Richard mused. 'Now I think of it, he looks rather like King Kong. Does he ever crash through?'

'He did once when I locked him in the bathroom,' said Daisy cheerfully, 'but the woodworm was bad in that door.'

'How's the woodworm upstairs?'

'I think that door should hold.'

'When we hear splintering wood,' said Richard, 'will it be too late to tell him we've signed a truce?' Daisy went to the bottom of the stairs and shouted,

'Be quiet, I'm ashamed of you!' and after another couple of thumps there was silence.

Richard was laughing, scratching behind Woo's ears, and she thought—the old papers didn't mention that the dark Lingards had a sense of the ridiculous. She caught herself up on that because she had just promised to treat Richard as an individual, not as the fifth dark Lingard. As an individual he would be a man she would like to know better.

He got up to leave. Daisy might have offered a cup of coffee if she hadn't been in her faded dressing gown, ready for bed. 'I like your cottage,' he said.

'Thank you.' The atmosphere of homeliness, like the furniture and the old prints on the wall, were all hers, her parents' and her grandparents', but she added, 'It isn't really mine, it's Uncle Bob's. It's an agricultural cottage, but it isn't needed for a farmworker.'

She opened the outer door and the cold air met her again

as Richard asked, 'Is there any other property attached to the farm?'

'About a dozen cottages.'

He patted Woo again, said, 'Explain to Cooch, will you, that I'm part of the family?'

'I will,' she said, and watched him go through the moonlight and the trees. Swiftly and silently, like a man with a hidden purpose.

Next morning Daisy drove her car out of the barn. Once the barn that was built on to the cottage had been filled with farming equipment, now all it did was garage one small mini, and as Daisy bumped on to the track she looked fleetingly towards the house. She felt better this morning. Richard Lingard would be having breakfast with the family, but she was determined to be sensible about him.

She told her colleagues in the library that a relation from America had turned up. It wasn't very surprising news, this was Shakespeare country and tourists who visited were often Americans. It was taken for granted that the relation was a holidaymaker. So in a way he was, on a working holiday, but Daisy didn't go into details. She said he seemed quite a nice man and left it at that.

She was out with Michael that evening, staying in town after work, and found herself unusually vague until he inquired if she was feeling off colour. She made an effort after that reproach and listened with the wide-eyed attention he expected while he talked about his troubles at work.

But all the time, whatever she was doing, there was this worrying undercurrent. Like a troublesome tooth, not really aching yet, just a niggle, a nag, a feeling that all was not well.

She hadn't been up to Oak House since Sunday, and on Tuesday as she turned her car off the track Alison came to the door of the cottage. Very occasionally Daisy did come home to find her sister here. But not often, Alison was usually too busy at Oak House. It was rare enough to make Daisy jump out of the car and hurry across and ask, 'Anything the matter?'

'Not really.' Daisy ignored the welcoming dogs. Alison wasn't her usual happy self, and Daisy held her in a comforting hug, giving her a little shake.

'Come on, out with it. Something's wrong.'

'Well——' Alison hesitated, then went on as though she was trying to laugh at herself, 'what you said on Sunday started it, about Richard muscling in, edging Keith out. It seemed crazy, but all the same I couldn't get it out of my mind.'

The strained smile went suddenly, leaving Alison's bright face in shadow. 'Yesterday,' she said huskily, 'I really began to wonder. And today, what's happened today.' Daisy felt a tiny tremor run through Alison as she still held her. 'Daisy,' Alison whispered, 'I'm scared you're right.'

CHAPTER FOUR

DAISY, with an arm still around Alison, led her sister back into the cottage. On the table was a half full mug of coffee, that Alison had been drinking when she'd heard Daisy's car coming, and Daisy said, 'Finish your coffee,' and went into the kitchen to turn on the kettle again and spoon instant coffee into a mug for herself.

The kettle boiled quickly and Daisy came back to Alison, put down her own mug of coffee and bent to pat Woo, who was working himself into a frenzy, terrified that he was being rejected.

'Now tell me what's happened,' said Daisy.

Alison took a deep breath and started on an unnaturally high note. 'It's to be expected, isn't it, that Richard should be interested in everything around here?' Daisy nodded. 'Yesterday,' Alison went on, 'he went out with Uncle Bob and Keith and asked questions about everything. How things worked, what the farm produces. He talked to the men—and got on very well with them, Keith says—and at lunchtime Uncle Bob was discussing the economic side of things with him.'

It must have been over the midday meal that Alison had begun looking at Richard, remembering what Daisy had said, feeling perhaps that he was concerning himself with matters that were not his province. 'It was quite a joke,' she said grimly. 'He apologised for being a bore, but he said he was getting a real kick, learning how his family lives.'

Smiling, Daisy had no doubt, using all that disarming charm. He would have noticed the glimmerings of suspicion in Alison's expression, and acted quickly to allay them. Just as he had tried to win Daisy round by wiping out her preconceived notions about dark Lingards.

'Then last night,' said Alison, 'Josh Warner came round.' Mr Warner was an old crony of Uncle Bob's, another farmer. 'And he had to meet Richard, of course. He remembered Andrew, they all went to school together. Well, you know how old Josh and Uncle Bob are, thick as thieves, chuntering to each other so that no one else can get a word in?' Daisy nodded again. 'But last night there were three of them puffing away round the fire,' said Alison, 'the two old boys with their pipes and Richard with a cigar. It's always been "young Keith", hasn't it, and Richard can't be all that much older than Keith, but Richard was right in there.'

Daisy had a swift dismaying impression of the scene. 'You know why Andrew took off for America?' Alison asked. Daisy didn't, so Alison related what she had heard last night. 'Because of a row he and Uncle Bob had over a girl. She jilted Uncle Bob as well and married somebody else, although it doesn't seem to have broken his heart, he couldn't remember her name until old Josh reminded him. But he and Andrew had quarrelled and from the way he looked at Richard when he said, "Maybe it still isn't too late to do something about that——" '

'Something about what?' Daisy interrupted.

'Andrew's share of the farm, perhaps?' Alison sounded fearful and she was, because if Uncle Bob should take it into his head to make Richard one of his heirs the future was grim. Keith's only hope of keeping their livelihood and their home going would be to inherit Oak House Farm unencumbered. Although Daisy had warned Alison that something like this might happen she instinctively tried to comfort her sister.

'It doesn't have to be the farm Uncle Bob was talking about. He might just mean he feels the quarrel is healed now he's seen Andrew's grandson.'

'You don't believe that's all Richard wants, do you, an old man's affection?' Alison said bitterly, and Daisy daren't answer, because she would have thought that simple affection was the last thing Richard Lingard wanted.

'Then today,' said Alison.

Of course, all that was yesterday, last night. Daisy had to hear about today yet. She took a gulp of scalding black coffee and Alison said, 'He didn't go out with them this morning. He walked around the house and finished up in the library. When I went in he was sitting at the table reading one of the books. He had his back to me and he didn't hear me, and when I spoke to him he barked, "Yes?"' She snapped out the word, and then smiled weakly. 'That doesn't sound much, does it?'

'It sounds sharpish,' said Daisy, and Alison went on quickly and defensively,

'I'm not over-touchy, am I? I mean, I don't expect to be handled with kid gloves all the time, but he sounded as if he owned the place and I was the one barging in. He was glaring at me for a moment. Then he said sorry, that he'd been miles away, but he scared me. That look, and the way he spoke.'

'A glimpse of the real Richard Lingard?' Daisy suggested. The dark Lingards had all had the devil's arrogance.

'If he'd ordered me to get out and stay out,' Alison could hardly believe what she was saying now, 'I would have crept away meek as a mouse. I felt I should have apologised for disturbing him.'

'What did happen?'

'I asked him if he wanted some coffee, that was what I'd gone in for, and he said no, thanks, he was going out.'

'Was he still annoyed?'

'Couldn't have been nicer. Like you say, it was just a glimpse.' She reached for her mug of coffee, and Daisy asked,

'Do you want anything stronger? There's some brandy in the cupboard.'

That made Alison smile naturally. 'This is strong enough, I'm not that shattered.' She sipped her coffee. 'And I feel much better now I've talked to you. It doesn't really add up to much, does it?'

'If I hadn't had a dark Lingard bee in my bonnet you wouldn't be thinking twice about any of it,' Daisy assured her.

They both drained their coffee mugs. 'You're not going out tonight, are you?' asked Alison.

'No.'

Alison laughed shakily, 'Then you can tell me if you think he's digging in.'

Richard returned to Oak House after the evening meal. They were all in the big kitchen when his car drew up by the stable block; and when Keith said, 'That sounds like Richard,' Uncle Bob said, 'Good,' as though the family had been incomplete before.

His footsteps in the passage seemed to Daisy to coincide with the thumping of her heart, that was suddenly loud in her ears. Then he opened the kitchen door, and although he had been on her mind almost all the time he was a shock all over again. She had forgotten how uneasy he made her feel.

She was helping to clear the table and she went on doing that, although Nanny was wanting to know whether he'd eaten or not. Yes, he said, he had, but Nanny wasn't satisfied. He was too thin, said Nanny, she didn't believe he'd been eating properly all these years, and he laughed and said that since he'd tasted the cooking in this house his problem was going to be keeping his weight down.

He wasn't too thin. Daisy looked up at him and quickly away again. There was no spare flesh on him, but he was wearing a thin black polo sweater and beneath it the rippling muscles of his shoulders showed.

'Keith's thinner,' Alison pointed out.

Keith was less muscular in spite of his outdoor life. He was a willowy young man, and although Nanny's ambition was to fatten up her menfolk until they were Uncle Bob's size she had become resigned to Keith eating heartily without gaining weight.

'Keith's always been puny,' sighed Nanny, and Alison shrilled indignantly,

'*Puny?*'

Only Daisy knew how sensitive Alison was right now to any criticism of Keith. Alison wasn't amused, although Keith grinned and warned Richard, 'She'll say the same about you if you don't put on a clear stone in the next fortnight.'

'Richard's got the bones,' said Nanny, as though most skeletons were plastic. 'He's got a big frame that ought to be carrying more flesh.'

Nanny's fussing was often funny, they often smiled at it, but this meant she was counting Richard one of her brood, and to Daisy and Alison that was no joke.

Beside Richard's hard handsome features Keith's face looked more boyish than ever, and Daisy was touched to see Alison put her hand on Keith's arm. She often did that. Their light quick caresses were the outward sign of their joy in each other, but this time it was more than affection Alison was showing, it was support. She was with Keith against Richard, although Keith had no suspicion that he was against Richard. He was as strong as he needed to be. He had hardly had a day's illness in his life, and he foresaw no trial of strength ahead.

Daisy looked across at Richard again, but meeting his dark eyes she blinked and almost backed off, and was angry with herself for showing his effect on her. She said, 'I hear you've been examining the old books.'

'Yes, I had a good morning's browsing.'

'They're not collector's items. The best isn't worth more

70

than a few pounds.' Her voice was honey-sweet. 'Books are my business.'

'Do you only price them?' he drawled. 'Or do you ever read any?' and while she seethed, seeking a cutting answer, 'Talking of work, I've got your photographs here.'

He took a cardboard folio out of the briefcase he had brought in with him, and large black and white prints from the folio. Even Uncle Bob was waiting to see how he had come out, only Daisy held back. She wanted to see her pictures, but she couldn't show eagerness.

Alison's stiffness dissolved at the first print Richard handed her. 'But this is lovely!' she gasped, and blushed slightly. 'I don't mean me, I mean the photograph. Look, isn't it smashing?' Alison was an attractive girl, but the photograph had made her gravely beautiful and they all admired it, and Keith said he'd be getting it framed.

'Hang on,' said Richard, 'until you've seen the others.'

All of them were good. Even the dogs, Cooch looked quite magnificent. Keith looked handsome and intelligent, and Alison was beautiful. Uncle Bob was full of character and Nanny's dignity and loving kindness brought a lump to your throat.

Daisy was pretty as a picture, and all her admirers would have been delighted with a copy, but she knew she could never force herself to ask for more.

There was plenty of discussion about which was everyone's best. Uncle Bob liked one of Daisy simpering. It wasn't a wide happy smile, she hadn't been happy, but she had smiled, and with her round face and her big eyes she said, 'I look like an old-fashioned chocolate box lid, but then I always do.'

'Soft centres?' asked Richard.

'That's our Daisy-girl,' said Uncle Bob, taking it as a compliment.

'How about this one?' Richard brought out the last print, of Daisy again, and she couldn't remember him taking it.

She hadn't been prepared and she wasn't smiling. She was frowning, her lips set, and there were shrieks of laughter from them all at the only candid camera shot in the pack.

'Put that on the chocolate box,' chuckled Keith, 'and they'd expect some hard centres!' He gave Daisy a brotherly hug. 'It's not right. Our Daisy-girl never looked like that.'

Richard Lingard thought otherwise, and she realised she was looking at him now with the same expression. He knew, what her nearest and dearest did not, that she was not all soft centre. She had a hard core, and with him around she needed to be tough.

'They are very good,' said Alison, looking at her own likenesses with a bemused expression.

'The best.' Keith was equally impressed.

'Not the best,' Richard contradicted, and Daisy blinked. She would have expected Richard to accept that tribute as no more than his due.

'I'm surprised you don't think so,' she said.

'Good enough to earn a living, but not good enough to make a fortune.'

As he snapped down the briefcase lock she asked, 'Do you want to make a fortune?'

'Who doesn't?' She didn't. A lot of people were satisfied with less than riches.

'Why? What for?' She was in dead earnest, but his grin mocked her sincerity.

'Power,' he said, leering like a melodrama villain so that they all laughed—even Alison, although she didn't look as happy as the others—but Daisy felt cold to her spine.

During the evening Daisy saw nothing that reassured her. In only two days Richard's position here had changed, subtly but surely. He moved around now, knowing his way as well as any of them, and anybody coming in here for the first time would have presumed he was closer to Uncle Bob than Keith was.

In all the years Daisy could hardly remember hearing

Uncle Bob ask Keith's advice. They worked the farm to-gether and Keith had a say in day-to-day matters, but the real decisions were always Uncle Bob's, and Keith accepted that—they all did. He was an old man, but too robust to seem old. Even his old-fashioned notions were vigorous and hearty.

He treated Richard as an equal, as a mature man. But so of course was Keith, and he was still 'young Keith' to Uncle Bob. Richard had travelled, he knew the world, and Uncle Bob asked him about things, and listened. Daisy never heard Richard actually giving any advice, but if he had done she felt that Uncle Bob might well have followed it.

Often in the evenings the two of them would sit, smoking and talking, and if Keith joined them he usually wandered out again, complaining that Uncle Bob was re-telling the tales of his youth, when Andrew was here.

Andrew must have been his favourite brother, and Richard was forging strong links. He was forging links everywhere. Friends and neighbours who met him were very impressed. If he had chosen he could have been on visiting terms with all of them, but he declined invitations, with courtesy and an underlying firmness that showed it would be a waste of time trying to make him change his mind.

When visitors came to Oak House Uncle Bob was ob-viously proud to introduce him, and although Alison fumed at the way Keith was put into second place Keith stayed good-humoured. He liked Richard. Richard was a good man and damned good company, and he would listen to no talk about a deliberate policy to get into Uncle Bob's good books and his will. Alison and Keith came as near as they ever had to a quarrel over that.

'He says it's rubbish,' Alison told Daisy.

'Well, it could be.' Daisy was needing reassurance as much as Alison these days; they were constantly telling each other that Richard wasn't ousting Keith, in spite of the evidence of their own eyes and ears. But even Keith couldn't pretend that Richard hadn't moved into Oak House.

He went off in the mornings with his camera, taking photographs to earn his living and looking at property, he said. When he returned to Oak House it was often with descriptions of houses he had seen and reasons why they weren't suitable. Sometimes he was away overnight, once for three days, and Uncle Bob and Nanny couldn't wait for him to come back.

The photographs were more successful than the house-hunting. He showed these to the family before he sent them off to his publishing contacts, giving copies when they were asked for. Uncle Bob and Nanny were collecting almost full sets, and sometimes Alison would ask for one, but Daisy never did. Not even when the place was a favourite spot.

The Dancing Stones were a collection of huge boulders from prehistory. No one knew who had put them there, or why or when. They topped a hill about ten miles away, and if you walked backwards round them on the nights of the old witch festivals all sorts of terrifying things were supposed to happen.

Daisy had never risked that, but she had had picnics there and it was a popular local spot for summer rambles, and when Richard produced a dozen or so photographs she was as intrigued as anyone. He had used light and shade in a fascinating way, bringing out patterns in the stones she had never seen before, and Nanny said, 'Daisy used to make up stories about the Dancing Stones when she was a girl.'

'Daisy used to make up stories about everything,' said Daisy.

'Including the dark Lingards,' said Richard.

'Of course, I came home to them.' She meant that they were part of Oak House, and an imaginative child, given

74

the run of the place, was bound to get involved in their strange saga.

Richard's face was as watchful as a hawk's. Not to you, she wanted to say, I would never come to you. But he had this tremendous personal magnetism and it almost seemed that he was willing her closer, which was crazy. She put both hands behind her back as he said, 'Do you want the photographs?'

'No, thank you,' she said. Not from him, not even a photograph, but when she saw that just discernible muscle move in his cheek she didn't know whether she was glad or sorry.

'Any luck with the house-hunting?' she asked.

'No.'

'Then I've something for you.' He had been looking at property from the advertisement in the *Post*, and if he saw saleboards up on his trips. He had gone about it very haphazardly, but although Daisy and Alison didn't much want him with a house in the district it would be better than having him living here in Oak House. So during her lunch hour today Daisy had called on the three estate agents in town, and collected details of everything on their books within his modest price range.

This should show whether he was serious about getting his own place, and Daisy didn't think he was. She dug into her handbag and brought out a wad of papers. Alison understood, but the rest took her gesture at surface value, they hoped she was trying to be helpful, although Uncle Bob stressed, 'There's no hurry,' and Nanny said,

'What's a single man like Richard need a house for that he won't be using half the time?' They both wanted Richard to stay on here, or at any rate to come back whenever he could and count it his home.

Daisy had put down the sheaf of stencilled papers on the table. Richard picked them up and leafed through them. 'Very thoughtful,' he said, with an amused and ironic glance at her. He wasn't fooled and she hadn't expected him to be. Alison looked at her gratefully but without hope, and Keith read over Richard's shoulder,

'The Old Mill at Woodmont. If they're only asking that much it must be in a state. In need of renovation? In need of rebuilding, more like.'

'I wouldn't mind something like that,' said Richard.

'Would you do it yourself?' Daisy inquired. There was no reason why he shouldn't be able to build a wall or reinforce a wooden beam, and she wasn't surprised when he said,

'Most of it.'

'Is there anything you can't do?' she asked tartly.

'Plenty of things.' He grinned wryly as though he had a backlog of failures, but she didn't believe him. He was not one of life's losers. Things went his way.

But he didn't buy the mill. That evening Daisy joined Alison in her never-ending task of home decoration. It wasn't as much fun as it used to be, before Richard came. But Alison still carried on, and Daisy and Nanny still helped her, and it was only when Daisy and Alison were alone that they voiced their fears that all their efforts might be for Richard Lingard's benefit.

It was hard grind keeping the farm going. Keith worked all hours, and here in Oak House Alison had very little leisure. She didn't complain, she hadn't an idle bone in her body. Nor was she greedy, she was generous to a fault. But Keith had earned his right to be master of Oak House Farm one day, and she had helped him earn it. Two masters—if Uncle Bob should be considering that—would be grossly unfair. And unworkable. Alison adored Keith, but she recognised Richard as immeasurably more forceful. In lots of ways she glimpsed the iron hand under that velvet glove, and she knew that even if Keith inherited the major part Richard would still be master.

But Keith only smiled when she tried to warn him, like

76

they had always smiled at Daisy and her dark Lingards. After that first near-quarrel Keith was treating Alison's suspicions so lightly that Alison stopped talking to him about Richard. She discussed Richard with no one but Daisy, and then she confined herself to a few words.

Tonight she said, 'Thanks for the dope on the houses for sale. Do you suppose he'll buy one?'

Daisy was down on her knees, painting a skirting board. She went on painting. 'I don't know.'

'But even if he does, 'said Alison, working on the opposite wall with a roller and a tray of pale coral paint, 'it won't make any difference to the way Uncle Bob feels about him. I can't see how anything's ever going to make any difference to that.' She stood back from the wall. 'I like this colour,' she said. 'Do you like this colour?'

'Yes,' said Daisy, 'I certainly do. There are some smashing colours about.'

They didn't mention Richard again, although they went on painting for another hour, chattering all the time.

That was how it always was, a brief shared frightened moment, followed by talk of something else. Both girls knew what was happening, but both were afraid to face it.

Nanny called them for supper, which was bread and cheese or cold meat and pickles, and as soon as everyone was round the kitchen table Uncle Bob announced, 'We've fixed Richard up with a place.'

How could they have done that, at this time of night? Daisy stared at Uncle Bob, who was beaming like a Toby jug, and then at Richard. 'The barn,' said Uncle Bob.

'What barn?' asked Alison.

'The barn on Daisy's cottage.'

'*My* barn?' It was no more Daisy's barn than it was her cottage, but her mind boggled at the thought of Richard moving into it. Of course he couldn't. It was just an old barn, nobody could live there. It had to be a joke, they were teasing her. She croaked, 'What could he do with my barn?'

'It shouldn't be hard to get planning permission,' said Keith, as though this was a feasible proposition. 'No problem with plumbing and electricity.' The cottage had main services, the barn was really part of the cottage. Daisy pleaded,

'You're all joking, aren't you?'

But they weren't. She looked at them and they weren't. Nanny said, 'I can't see why he can't stay where he is, but it seems all the fashion these days, doing up barns, doing up all sorts of funny places.'

No! Daisy wanted to shout. I don't want him the other side of my wall, I couldn't bear him being so close to me. She said, 'I think it's a rotten idea. It would cost a fortune to heat, it's just a big empty space right up to the rafters, and it would cost another fortune to fix so that anyone could live in it.'

Richard sat, chin in hand, reflectively calm. 'It has a gallery and the living space could be open plan. I reckon I could convert it. Put in a dark room. I think it would suit me very well.'

He had been prowling around, he knew the layout of the barn. He probably had the blueprint for reconstruction in his head. He'd never had any intention of buying a house, and there wasn't a free cottage going, so he had settled for the barn. 'An old Cotswold stone barn with great potential,' was how the estate agents would have described it, and Uncle Bob was handing it to him. Daisy said coldly, 'I'd hate to have a neighbour. Why can't you find a barn somewhere else?'

'There isn't another barn empty,' Keith pointed out. Not on Oak House Farm land, not for free, but he could have found one if he'd been prepared to pay for one. She knew she was looking sullen, she was scared that her lips might tremble unless she kept them tight together, and tension cut a scowl between her brows.

Richard said quietly, 'If it would worry you having me

78

next door then of course I'll look for somewhere else.'

'You will not.' Uncle Bob was laying down the law, in a voice that was never challenged in this house. 'You'll have that barn. It worries all of us, Daisy being on her own in that cottage. One of the family next door to her would be a burden off my mind, so let's hear no more about her not wanting a neighbour.'

She wouldn't have minded a neighbour, she might have welcomed one, but not Richard. Her objections were only to Richard, but Uncle Bob would uphold no appeal against him. This showed how strongly Uncle Bob felt about Richard being accepted as a permanent member of the household, and he would never admit that this might be unfair to Keith.

'You can garage your car up here, Daisy,' said Uncle Bob. 'And while summer lasts it won't hurt to let it stand out.'

Garaging my car, thought Daisy grimly, is the least of my worries! She nodded, she couldn't trust herself to speak, and from then on she tried to shut her ears to the men talking.

Alison was quiet too. She was quieter these days when Richard was around. Nanny said she needed a holiday and Keith would have arranged one for her—he couldn't get away himself, harvest time was coming up—but Alison wouldn't hear of it. As she said to Daisy, 'I wouldn't have a minute's peace away from here, I'd be wondering what was going on all the time.'

As soon as Daisy reasonably could she said goodnight, and as she got up from the table Richard did too. 'May I walk back with you?' he asked.

'Do you want to take another look at your barn?'

'I want a walk.'

The dogs were on their feet, close behind her, and Richard was behind her too, out of the kitchen, down the passage, through the back door. She walked fast, until she

79

realised how ridiculous it was trying to outpace him, then she slowed to her normal pace and ignored him, watching Woo darting from side to side of the track, and Cooch stomping steadily on.

Richard said, 'It's a waste of a good barn. Why not turn it into a house?'

'No reason.'

'Except that you don't want a neighbour?'

'I prefer being on my own.' She was trying to keep personalities out of this, it was more dignified that way. 'Whatever Uncle Bob says, I don't need protecting, and if I did——' The last four words slipped out, and of course he wanted the sentence completed.

'If you did?' he prompted.

After a moment, while she considered keeping her mouth shut for the remaining minute it should take to reach the cottage, she told him flatly, 'Somehow I don't see you as a protector. More as a predator.'

He walked like a black panther and she wanted to get into her cottage. She opened her handbag for the key, so that she need waste no time when they reached the door. 'And what am I supposed to be preying on?' he asked.

At the door, as she slipped the key in the lock, he put his hand over her hand, not gripping, just stopping her from turning the key. 'Tell me,' he said. She felt his light touch like talons in her soft flesh and stifled a cry. Biting her lips, she said,

'Another thing I don't see, you settling for a barn.'

He had a small stake here now, but he wanted more than that and he was going about getting it. He was preying on them all. As he took his hand away she turned the key and pushed the door, and she could hear him laughing. 'Goodnight, neighbour,' he said.

When she came home from work next day they were working on the barn. It had been cleared out, the walls were being whitened inside, and before another week was over a couple of windows had been made. Richard bought a Calor gas fire, and a couple of paraffin heaters, and with a bed, a table and some chairs from the farm, the barn was habitable enough to camp out in.

He had been up in London for a couple of days, seeing his agent, and Daisy waited his return with trepidation. So far he hadn't slept down here, and she had a premonition that she wouldn't sleep so well herself when he was on the other side of that wall during the night.

She did sleep, of course. She was young and healthy and tired, but she resented him being there, and when she got into her car next morning it annoyed her to see his car parked beside it. He came out of the barn and said, 'Good morning. Do you want the dogs taken up to the house?'

Alison or Nanny collected the dogs some time during the morning, after which they had the run of the kitchen and around the farm until Daisy came home in the evenings. She said, 'I don't think Cooch would go with you.'

'Shall we try him?'

She nearly said, 'I don't have time, I'm late,' but she obviously wasn't late, so she had to get out of the car and open the cottage door, then watch with hardly hidden chagrin while not only the terrier but the peke too greeted Richard. Cooch always knew how she felt about people, so why wasn't he snarling at Richard who was taking the liberty of patting him?

Richard looked up at her. 'He doesn't bite me and I won't bite him.'

'A good slogan.' She had to smile.

'Try it some time,' he said.

Daisy had never used her cottage much for entertaining. Men got the wrong idea when they were invited home by a girl who lived alone in a small wood, so that her home-cooked dinners were usually for foursomes, Keith and Alison were her standbys. Since Richard arrived she hadn't had the heart for dinner parties, but when dates brought

81

her home or collected her they weren't pleased to find the barn occupied, and Daisy was getting tired of insisting that it had nothing whatever to do with her.

It might have been the expensive car that irritated them, but the briefest glimpse of Richard Lingard seemed to bring out suspicion in men whom she would have expected to have more sense. 'Who the hell's that?' they usually asked.

'Richard Lingard,' she'd say. 'A relation. Uncle Bob's given him the barn. He's converting it.'

'He's going to live in it? Right next to you?'

'Yes.'

They didn't like that. Neither did Daisy, especially as Richard was finding the situation amusing. It was a good summer, the evenings were warm and fine, and when he was there in the evenings his door was usually open so that if anyone called at Daisy's cottage he saw them, and they saw him. Sometimes he waved her goodbye. Sometimes he sauntered over and she had to introduce him.

She had three weeks of that, and then Michael brought her home from an evening out, and she asked him in for a coffee. Things had been strained between her and Michael lately. She couldn't explain what was happening at Oak House Farm, but he knew that Daisy was preoccupied and not with him, and that made him peevish.

She had perked coffee and put a brandy beside him when someone knocked on the door. Woo barked, but Cooch wagged his tail so she was afraid it was going to be Richard, and it was. 'Everything all right?' he asked.

'Yes, of course everything's all right.'

'Hello.' Richard looked beyond her at Michael, whom he had met the week before outside the cottage. 'Sorry to interrupt, but I heard voices, and you never know these days, do you?'

Michael was taken aback, but he agreed that these days you did not know.

'Goodnight,' said Richard, as Daisy closed the door with a slight slam, and Michael said thoughtfully,

'I suppose it is better for you, somebody living next door. It's lonely here.'

'Not any more it isn't,' said Daisy ruefully. Michael's car was in the drive. It wasn't a distinctive model, but Richard would remember whose it was, and he would know who was in the cottage. He wasn't doing this because he considered her a helpless female but because it amused him to rile her, and she was riled.

'Does he always come round if he hears anyone in here?' Michael was asking. There hadn't been any visitors after dark since Richard moved into the barn, but Daisy could have said, 'Yes,' because she was almost sure he was going to.

She said, 'It's Uncle Bob's idea. They've never liked me living alone, they've always wanted me to go and live at the house, and Richard being next door was supposed to be a —protection.'

The word stuck, and Michael said, 'Why don't you want to live at the house?'

'Because I like my cottage.' Until three weeks ago. But now she couldn't even bring back a friend without being inspected and embarrassed. It was worse than Uncle Bob's cross-questioning of her boy-friends. Uncle Bob was genuinely concerned for her, but if she was living at Oak House she might easily get more privacy than she was getting here.

She sat down, on a chair, not on the sofa beside Michael, her hands clasped tightly around her knees. Now there was a thought. If she left this cottage Uncle Bob would probably let Richard have it, then he could turn the barn into a studio, and he'd have a super home.

He could be trying to hound her out. He knew she didn't want him living so close and he was making things as uncomfortable as possible for her. Suspicion hardened into certainty and with that on her mind she looked so tense that Michael believed her when she said she was very tired.

Daisy didn't object when he said, 'I'll be off, then.' She shot to her feet and saw him out, shutting the door instead of walking to his car with him. Behind her, as she closed the door, Cooch had growled softly at him. The dog had not growled at Richard Lingard, Michael recalled. In fact it had acted as though Richard was a welcome caller.

Daisy didn't hear the car drive away, she was so wrapped up in her own indignation. Of *course* Richard wanted the cottage, and he thought if he kept this up she'd get so rattled that she would simply clear out and go and live in the big house. He had a hope. But she wasn't having him acting as though he was here to keep an eye on her.

Uncle Bob had given him the barn, and so far as Uncle Bob was concerned Richard could do no wrong. But they had always said that Daisy could twist Uncle Bob round her little finger, and tomorrow she would tell him how difficult it was, ask him to ask Richard to stop pestering her.

She went up to the house next morning, before she went to work. Alison was the only one in the kitchen, washing up the breakfast things. 'Is Uncle Bob around?' Daisy asked.

'I think he's in the study—why?' Alison looked as though she hadn't slept well either, and as Daisy explained she sighed.

'It's all worry, isn't it? You'd better hurry or you won't catch him, he's off down town.'

In the study Uncle Bob looked up from papers on the desk to smile broadly at Daisy. 'Here's an early bird. Has your car broken down? Are you after a lift?'

She came across to him. 'I want to talk to you, please, if you've got the time.'

The jovial creases in his big red face settled into serious lines, and he settled back in his chair. 'I've always got time for you, my dear. You should know that by now.'

Of course she knew it, and she loved this strong, stubborn old man, and she was sure he would understand what she had to tell him. There was no point trying to explain why she felt that Richard was usurping Keith's rightful role. On that Robert Lingard's mind was closed. But this was a simple matter, just upsetting for Daisy, and Uncle Bob could put it right for her.

She said, 'I wish you'd talk to Richard and tell him I don't need a round-the-clock watch on me.' That was an exaggeration. Richard was away much longer hours than she was, but even when he wasn't in the barn she could imagine him behind the dark windows. And in her own cottage she often looked at that dividing wall, as conscious of him on the other side as though she could see through stone.

Uncle Bob nodded as she talked, with the occasional non-committal grunt. Once started she ran on, recounting every time Richard had happened to be outside or with the door open when anyone came to call for her, and then last night, and Michael . . .

'Wasn't it late to be asking the young man in?' interposed Uncle Bob, who didn't really approve of young ladies issuing invitations, and certainly not after dusk. Daisy defended herself,

'It wasn't that late, and I know Michael very well.'

'All the same——' The phone rang, and stopped ringing almost at once, and Uncle Bob frowned at it, needing a moment or two to reconnect his argument. 'All the same, I don't think we should complain about Richard making sure you were all right.'

'Well, next time,' said Daisy, 'would you ask him please to look first and see if there's a car outside?' Of course he had known there was a car, and whose car it was. 'And would you ask him not to come out every time. Or to keep away from the window because——' her voice shot out of control into a squeak of exasperation, 'because he's putting my friends off. They think I had something to do with getting him into that barn, and he's acting like some sort of watchdog!'

Uncle Bob rumbled with laughter and Daisy could have wept. She pleaded, 'Won't you just tell him I don't need protecting and I don't want watching?'

'I'll have a word with him,' he promised, and she hoped for the best. After a word from Uncle Bob, even if it was jocular, Richard might keep more in the background. She would always know he was there, but perhaps he wouldn't come knocking at her door.

She watched Uncle Bob drive away; she had allowed herself plenty of time, so she could have a few minutes with Alison before she got into her own car to go to work.

Nanny came bustling out of the house, waving a duster and glaring down the drive at Uncle Bob's rapidly vanishing shooting-brake. 'Was that the master?' she demanded of Daisy.

'Yes.'

'I thought he'd gone ages ago.' Nanny tutted as though somebody was to blame for this. If there was any blame it was Daisy's, so Daisy said,

'I was talking to him. Did you want him?'

'There was a phone call a few minutes back, when I was by the phone in the hall. Mr Laurenson's got the 'flu and he can't see him.'

'Well, he'll know when he gets there,' said Daisy. Alison had walked out behind Nanny.

'The appointment was mid-morning. He's getting some new boots first, so it won't be a wasted journey,' Alison said quietly.

Nanny went back into the house and Alison said, 'We have a reprieve.'

'What?'

Alison's hands were hanging limply and her shoulders were drooping. She looked very tired. 'You know who Mr Laurenson is—Uncle Bob's lawyer. Uncle Bob was going to see him this morning about changing his will.'

'Oh no!' Daisy whispered.

'Fair shares,' said Alison. 'Half and half. Keith and Richard.'

'Oh, he *wouldn't*!'

'Not this morning. Unless someone else will do as well to make out a new will. If it has to be Mr Laurenson we've got another few days.' A flicker of life was creeping into her voice. She looked at Daisy with desperate eyes, and Daisy asked with matching desperation,

'What can we do? What does Keith think about it?'

The dogs were ambling around the courtyard, but at the sound of Daisy's voice Cooch had stopped snuffling and was now padding across.

'Keith can't do anything,' said Alison. 'He doesn't stand a chance against Richard. He might as well go and batter that wall, Richard's as hard as they come. But if he does have a weak spot, then it's got to be you, Daisy.'

CHAPTER FIVE

THE idea of her being Richard Lingard's weakness almost made Daisy smile. But of course there was nothing to smile at. 'Are you sure about the will?' she asked Alison. 'Did Uncle Bob tell you? What did he say?'

Cooch had reached her by now, and was standing very close and still, looking up at her. There was no one around. The courtyard could fill any minute, work on the farm had already started for the day, but for the moment the sisters were alone, although Alison glanced around and up at the windows of the house before she answered.

Even then she spoke in hardly more than a whisper. 'I heard him telling Richard. I was in the laundry room and they were in the kitchen, and Uncle Bob said, 'I'm seeing Laurenson at eleven o'clock in the morning and having everything divided equally between you and Keith.'

Alison was white-faced. She hadn't put on any make-up this morning, not even a touch of lipstick. She said, 'I didn't hear any more, they both went out into the passage. I told Keith and he knows there's nothing he can do, but it isn't *fair*, is it?'

'No,' said Daisy, '*no*!'

'At breakfast Uncle Bob said he was going into town to get some boots, and he said I didn't look well and Keith ought to make me take that holiday.' Alison was biting her lip, holding back tears, and Daisy put an arm around her trembling sister, her own blood hot with anger.

It seemed that no one dared speak out against Richard. Keith was scared that if he did he might find himself out of

Uncle Bob's favour altogether, and Keith was really no fighter. Alison was afraid for Keith, but Daisy said, 'I can't believe that Uncle Bob could be so underhand. I shall tell him what I think about this, but I still can't believe it of him.'

'It isn't Uncle Bob's fault,' said Alison. 'It's Richard's influence. There is a curse, you know. The dark Lingards are a curse. If only you'd left them alone Richard would never have come here.'

Daisy knew that. She would never forgive herself for writing that article.

A couple of men called 'Morning!' across the yard, and both girls managed to answer in fairly normal tones. Then the girls began to walk away, down the drive towards the cottage and the road, so that it looked as if they were gossiping instead of wondering how to face a situation that meant the disruption of their lives.

The only sign was in the peke, trotting closer than usual to Daisy's heels. Alison said, 'You've got to help me.'

'How?'

'I've been thinking about it all night. I didn't get much rest. I don't think Keith did either, but he pretended he was asleep.' Alison's natural voice was warm and lively, full of light and laughter, but this morning there was no life in it. 'Richard fancies you,' she went on.

'Never!'

'This antagonism between you, the way you keep snapping at him—perhaps it's a challenge to him, but he can't keep his eyes off you. I've noticed that, and now this business with the cottage, scaring the other men off.'

'That's because he wants the cottage.'

'I think he wants you,' said Alison, and while Daisy was still speechless, 'Most men do, don't they?' Daisy was attractive to most men, bees to the honeypot, but she had always thought there was mutual hostility between herself and Richard. 'I'm not saying he's in love with you,' said

89

Alison wearily. 'Just that he fancies you.'

That was possible. 'Even if he does,' said Daisy, very far from convinced, 'how could it help? What do you want me to do? Ask him to tell Uncle Bob he doesn't want half the farm?'

That was impossible. She felt instinctively that no one could influence Richard Lingard against his own interests.

They were walking side by side, and when Alison stumbled very slightly Daisy realised that her sister's eyes were closed, the face shuttered in sadness, tears forcing their way beneath the dark lashes.

'Richard is going to get this place,' whispered Alison. 'He just walks in and it's going to be his because he will tell Keith what to do. He won't take orders, he'll give them.'

She stood still, in the middle of the track, her eyes still shut. 'I mustn't start crying,' she sounded panicky. 'If anybody sees me what can I tell them?' She sniffed and blinked, dabbing damp cheeks with the back of her hand. 'Can we get into the cottage without him coming out?'

There was no sign of Richard's car beside Daisy's little Mini, with the painted daisy on the door, and the two girls hurried inside. Daisy said bitterly, 'This used to be a real refuge before Uncle Bob put him on the other side of that wall. Are you all right?'

Alison was not all right, she was in despair, but she nodded, and sniffed again and glared at the wall, although as Richard's car had gone Richard was unlikely to be in the barn. Perhaps at eleven o'clock he would be meeting Uncle Bob at the solicitor's office, and suggesting that a routine task like changing a will could be handled by anyone who could take down dictation.

'Some protection!' said Daisy savagely. 'I should think he's about the most dangerous man I've ever met.'

'But that's it. That's my idea.' Alison sounded diffident as a child afraid of being laughed at. Her confidence had been sapped lately, she could only clutch at straws. 'Well, you know how strait-laced Uncle Bob is.' She spoke slowly, watching Daisy's reaction. 'So far Richard can do no wrong, but if Uncle Bob knew that he'd made a pass at you, a real pass, it might dawn on him that Richard's no knight in shining armour.'

Daisy began to frown. That would be playing with fire, and asking to get burned. She couldn't see herself as a calculating seductress.

'You've always been Uncle Bob's pet,' Alison reminded her. 'Sometimes I think he's fonder of you than he is of Keith even. If it looked as though Richard was trying it on with you Uncle Bob might realise he isn't completely trust-worthy.'

It sounded a simple plan, but it was riddled with pitfalls. 'I couldn't!' Daisy's hands moved instinctively as though she pushed the idea, or Richard Lingard, away from her; and Alison sat in the button-backed chair that had been her favourite seat as a girl in this cottage, huddling down, press-ing her face into a cushion so that her voice was muffled.

'If he gets half the farm, Daisy, it's the finish. You know how things are, there isn't the money there. We'd have to sell the house, and who'd buy a place like this these days, and it isn't fair. It belongs to Keith and me. And our children.'

Daisy knelt down beside her, remembering four years ago, after their father's death when they had been alone to-gether like this. Since then there had been no tears, and perhaps too much contentment.

I hate him, thought Daisy. Uncle Bob can't see that he's an opportunist who'll take all he can get and give back nothing. To Keith and Alison, the old house, and the land it stood on, were a trust, to cherish and succour. Richard Lingard would drain it, pocket the proceeds and move on.

Uncle Bob loved Daisy, she was his pet, but he wouldn't believe her if she told him that Richard was a predator. She would have to show it beyond all doubt, and the surest way might be to set herself up as prey.

There was a sour taste in her mouth as she said, 'You want me to—lead Richard on?' and Alison looked up from the cushion, hoping a little.

'You wouldn't have to do much. Just give him a chance and he'll take it.'

Daisy had had plenty of experience in handling importunate lovers, but she hadn't led any of them on. She was kind and she wasn't a fool. She said ironically, 'Then I say, "sorry, but I've changed my mind"? Suppose, just suppose, I can't stop him?'

Alison shrank from the thought of putting Daisy in any sort of danger, but she would almost have died herself to keep Oak House for Keith. She said, 'There'd have to be someone within earshot.'

'Then I scream "Rape"?' Daisy was near to hysterical laughter. 'Shall you expect me to press charges?' It was a wholly distasteful scheme, but Alison said quickly,

'Of course you wouldn't let it get that far.'

'I—don't like it.' That was putting it mildly, when her skin was crawling on her bones.

'Nor do I.' Alison's eyes were glittering with unshed tears, her voice was brittle. 'I hate it. It's a mean trick and it's not nice being mean. So what do we do? Nothing? We let him take our home and our living and—everything?'

Not if I can help it, Daisy thought. This is my fault, it has to be my battle, and if I must fight him what other weapon do I have?

Alison read the indecision in Daisy's face and pleaded, 'It isn't as though we'd be lying about him. He's got to be a womaniser. He certainly isn't frustrated, and a man with his sex appeal who isn't married at his age must be playing the field and enjoying it. He doesn't fancy me or I swear I'd get him to make a pass, just to show Uncle Bob the kind of man he is.'

She wasn't talking wildly, she was working out a desperate plan that might work. 'He'd seduce you if he got the chance,' she said. 'Well, of course we don't give him the chance, but we let Uncle Bob know that he tried.'

Daisy shook her head. She badly wanted to refuse. In her heart she knew that she couldn't, but she went on shaking her head, and Alison's calm broke and she grabbed Daisy's hands, tears pouring down her cheeks, begging, 'Please, Daisy, *please*!'

'I'll—think about it,' said Daisy. 'You must let me think about it.'

'Yes, of course.' Alison still clung to her and Daisy felt old.

'Don't cry,' she said. 'I brought him here, I'll get rid of him.' She meant it. Somehow. 'But give me a little time,' she said, 'to see if I can think of any other way.'

She thought about it all morning, doing her work almost automatically, but there was no other way, and as Alison had said, they wouldn't be lying about Richard if they showed him up in his true colours. Dear Uncle Bob was one of the last of the Victorian patriarchs, with a sturdy Puritan streak so far as his women were concerned.

The permissive age was anathema to him, but Richard Lingard was very much a part of it. If Daisy stopped being aggressive and played up to Richard it was more than likely that he would try to make love to her, and if Uncle Bob believed that Daisy hadn't wanted that—and she most emphatically did not—and hadn't expected it, he would be shocked and angry. It might radically change his ideas about Richard.

Alison phoned her at work during the afternoon. 'Daisy? Have you thought of any other way?'

'No.'

'Will you do it?'

'Yes.'

'Bless you! See you this evening.'

'We'd better get together on our plan of action,' said

Daisy, and Alison laughed shakily,

'We sound like a pair of conspirators!'

'What else are we?' asked Daisy.

Richard was not in the barn when Daisy went up to the house that evening, where she watched television with Nanny and Keith and Alison. Uncle Bob had old Josh round and they missed Richard. Old Josh asked after him, and Uncle Bob said he was fine and he might be strolling up later.

If he had done Daisy would have been amiable, not conspicuously so, but like she was with everyone else. That was the plan. Alison was convinced that Richard would make the running soon enough. But he didn't come, and after supper Alison walked back to the cottage with Daisy, and there was still no sign of his car.

'Maybe he's away overnight,' said Alison.

Daisy hoped so, but it wasn't very late yet, he could still turn up. Tomorrow she would start being neighbourly. She'd say good morning and smile. Big deal, she thought, but she had never been a hypocrite and she felt a wave of self-disgust before she'd even started. Goodness knows how she would feel if she brought this off.

She said, 'I hope I can do it. He could turn me down.'

'Not a chance. He's out for all he can get,' said Alison bitterly.

Uncle Bob hadn't said why he wanted to see his solicitor this morning. They didn't know whether he had changed his will yet or if he was waiting for Mr Laurenson to recover from the 'flu, but they both knew that it was Richard's company the two old farmers had missed tonight. There had been no suggestion that Keith might join them while they set the world straight, smoking their pipes and drinking their strong ale, in front of the fire in the small sitting room.

Daisy wandered around her living room and kitchen. There wasn't much for her to do, but she was too strung up for sleep. She had let herself in for what could be a very humiliating scene, because she didn't share Alison's certainty that Richard found her all that physically attractive.

Alison had been exaggerating when she said he couldn't keep his eyes off Daisy. He wasn't going to do anything that would cause trouble, so Daisy might have to go a fair way to meet him. A smile and a good morning wouldn't have him grabbing her. Not unless the smile was both promising and provoking, and up to now Daisy's allure had been her little-girl artlessness. It was all she usually needed to have men eating out of her hand, but if she fluttered the long lashes of the big blue eyes at Richard Lingard he would know she was acting. He had recognised the tough core in her, the mature woman. He had taken that simpering photograph of her, but the one he had taken when she was unaware she was being photographed had shown another face. The two faces of Daisy Penrose sounded like the title of a book. Two-faced meant playing false, being a double-dealer, and she hadn't had much practice in deceit, and Richard would be a hard man to cheat.

'You'll only have to lead him on a little,' Alison had said, but Daisy had a suspicion that he might prove canny, committing himself no further than she did herself. And if it went that way of course it was no go. Since he was living next door she had been much more jittery than when her cottage was isolated, but now she was expected to entice him into an explosive sexual situation she was terrified.

In daylight, and with Alison, it hadn't seemed so bad, but all alone now she whispered, 'I can't, I *can't*!' and Cooch whimpered, the huge dark liquid eyes fixed on her. Then his ears lifted a fraction and seconds later Woo and Daisy heard the car too.

It stopped, so it was Richard. If she opened the door and stepped outside now she would have made the first important move. But if she left it till morning she would be admitting to herself that it was probably beyond her, and it would be twice as hard.

She opened the door and the two dogs shot out. She said stupidly, 'It *is* you.'

'Hello,' he said, and to Cooch, 'hello, boy.' Woo danced around, a spot of flickering whiteness, and Richard called him closer and patted him too.

Daisy said, 'You're the only new friend Cooch has made in five years.'

'Five years?'

'That's how old he is. Until now he hasn't wanted to know unless he's known you all his life. Perhaps he's getting less selective in his old age.'

Richard laughed. 'On a ratio of one year in a dog's life equalling seven he's not much over my age. We've got a lot in common, we're both into a very selective senility.'

That, and her nervousness, kept her giggling, and as he walked from the car towards his door she said, 'Can you spare a minute?'

'Any number.' She went into her house and he followed. She said,

'This morning I asked Uncle Bob if he'd tell you I don't need protecting.' It wouldn't rank as a friendly gesture if Uncle Bob got this in before Daisy did. If she told it she could soften it into a joke against herself. She grimaced, 'But he said you were quite right to come round and make sure I wasn't being mugged.'

'But you'd rather I didn't?'

'Well, yes. Although as we are neighbours we might as well be friends.' He was still in the doorway and she twisted her hands nervously.

The hooded eyes told her nothing. She almost expected him to say, 'And what exactly is your game?' and a wretched betraying blush stained her fair skin. Then he said quietly, 'There is nothing I would like better.' His smile wasn't cynical, although it was the crooked smile. 'Shall we drink

96

to it?' he said. 'Can I bring a bottle of wine round? I'd invite you to my place, but I only have one chair.'

She nodded mutely and the moment he had gone panicked. She hadn't contemplated an immediate get-together. Suppose he took all this as meaning she was amenable to overtures? That was the impression she had to give, but not until she and Alison had set the scene. He was a man of the world, and last night she had been entertaining Michael in here, and during the last three weeks she had had other dates. Maybe he thought she was easy. A man like Richard Lingard probably didn't believe in twenty-two-year-old virgins.

When he walked back into the room carrying a bottle of wine she said, 'I'm not much of a drinker.'

'That's all right,' he said, 'it's not much of a wine.' He went into the kitchen and found a couple of glasses while she still stood around. Then he opened the bottle and poured out, handed her a glass, and seated himself in an armchair.

Daisy almost sat on the sofa, then realised that might seem like an invitation, and went to the little yellow button-backed chair instead; and although she had seen Richard's charm in action before she was grateful for it now. She sat, cradling her glass, and he did the talking, and none of it was personal so that her tension eased, and she laughed because he was funny, and after ten minutes or so she was talking too.

He asked about the book she had been writing and she said, 'There's an old brown leather case in the attics at Oak House and some of the Lingard papers and my manuscript are in it. I've given up.'

'Because I turned up?'

She nodded, 'Partly.' More than partly. She didn't know why she hadn't burned the wretched book that had been the cause of all their troubles, and when Richard asked,

'May I read it?' she demurred,

97

'I don't think it was very good.'

'I'll be surprised if it isn't. Would you object to me reading it?'

'As you've shown us your work I don't see how I can object.' She smiled, 'Nor do I see how I can stop you, the case isn't locked.'

'Is that your ambition, to be a writer?'

'I enjoy writing, and I love working among books.' Some day of course she wanted to marry and live here so that her children and Alison's could grow up together. Almost as though he followed her thoughts Richard asked,

'Do your future plans include any of the men I've met?'

He had met three of Daisy's dates, including Michael, and she had no real involvement with any of them. She wished now that there was a man in whom she could confide, so that she would not be fighting Richard alone. 'Only as friends,' she said, and as he seemed sceptical, 'don't you believe in friendship between men and women?'

'Why not?' He looked at her in a way that had her heart hammering. 'But I can't see how the thoughts of any man going around with you could stay platonic for long.'

She laughed at that, blushing, and he said, 'The photographs I took of you didn't do you justice. What are you doing tomorrow?'

Tomorrow was Sunday. 'Why?' She was supposed to be going to a party, but nothing was as important as playing this farce out as quickly as possible.

'We could go out for the day and I could take some more shots of you.'

'I do have a date,' she said, 'but I could cancel it.'

'Good.' Richard drained his glass. 'Ten o'clock all right?'

'Where shall we go?'

'Does it matter?'

'No,' she said, 'so long as we're not too late getting back.'

'Goodnight, then.' Daisy didn't move from her seat. She just said,

'Goodnight,' and when the door closed behind her she drank the rest of the wine in her glass, from which until now she had only taken a few sips. The bottle on the table was still three-quarters full, and she managed at last to re-place the cork. It wasn't easy, the way her hands were shaking. When they came back tomorrow they would come in here and she would produce the bottle and supper, and everything should work out according to plan.

Alison was right. Richard did find her physically desir-able. He did want her. He would have kissed her tonight if she had gone towards him. So why hadn't she? That might almost have been enough to get him into Uncle Bob's bad books if she could have acted her part of outraged innocence realistically.

But no, it wouldn't have been enough. Not a simple kiss. It had to be more than that. It had to look like an—assault, and either tomorrow night or not at all, because Daisy couldn't stand it any longer.

She was shaking from head to foot. Anyone would think she *had* been assaulted. The peke whined and she said, 'You snarl at the harmless ones and you make friends with the enemy. You're letting me down after all these years.'

But what she and Alison were doing wasn't a joke, and because she hadn't any sleeping pills, and because she knew she wouldn't fall asleep naturally, she took three aspirins with hot milk and tried to blot tomorrow from her mind in their resulting drowsiness.

She woke with her head aching, gripped by a vague nausea. I'm ill, she thought. But she was never ill, she was healthy peasant stock, and the only thing wrong with her now was that she didn't want to spend today with Rich-ard, much less tonight. She wanted to plead she was ill and couldn't come. But she wasn't really sick, just scared.

It was eight o'clock, and as lying here worrying wouldn't make things any easier she got up. There were all the signs of a day of sunshine ahead, and she put on a denim skirt and a soft pink cheesecloth blouse, matched by a deep rose lipstick, and crept out of the cottage, closing her door quietly.

Woo began to bark his head off as soon as he got outside, but the barn door stayed closed and Richard didn't appear, and Daisy walked fast up the track towards the farmhouse.

How she loved this house that had been so inextricably a part of her life! Now it was threatened its beauty became poignant and piercing so that her eyes misted as she neared it.

It was incredible that Uncle Bob didn't realise that joint heirs could mean the end of Oak House Farm as it had stood over the centuries. But Uncle Bob was an old man, and Richard was the grandson of the brother he had loved best, and he believed that he could trust Richard. Today Daisy would undeceive him on that.

Breakfast was later on Sundays, but everyone was stirring. She said hello to Nanny and Uncle Bob in the kitchen, and told them she was going out with Richard so that he could take some more photographs of her. That pleased them. They were smiling about that when she went to find Alison.

She met a dour-faced Keith on the stairs and asked impulsively, 'Have you spoken to Uncle Bob about carving up the farm?'

'What's the use?' He sighed deeply. 'You've seen how he is about Richard.'

I see what's happening to you and Alison, thought Daisy, torn with pity. She said grimly, 'Yes, I do see. Is Alison up?'

Alison was dressing in the bedroom and she raised a smile for Daisy. 'You look nice. Is that a new lipstick?'

'Not very. Are you going to put some lipstick on today?'

'Why not?' Alison grimaced at herself in the mirror. 'I feel rotten, but life goes on.'

'I didn't feel too good either when I first woke up,' Daisy

100

admitted, 'only that was because I'm spending today with Richard.' She plonked herself down on the unmade bed. 'We had a chat last night and you're right, he does fancy me.'

To a man like Richard a girl probably was one of life's small pleasures, like an old brandy or a good cigar. To Richard Lingard she was fanciable.

Alison had been zipping up her skirt. She frowned, head bent, looking up at Daisy. 'Did he——?'

'No,' said Daisy with laboured lightness. 'It was late and perhaps he'd had a busy day. But he will when we get back tonight. He doesn't waste time, he's a fast worker. So I'll leave the dogs here.' Woo had stayed in the kitchen, cadging titbits from Nanny, but Cooch was with her. 'Will you walk them down to the cottage about nine?' Alison nodded. 'Then I can tell you what nearly happened,' said Daisy.

'And I'll tell Uncle Bob.' Daisy winced, and Alison was shocked by the over-eagerness in her own voice. She felt almost as badly as Daisy about this, but she reasoned that Richard was using all his charm to influence Uncle Bob, so what was wrong in showing the other side of the coin, the selfish and sensual side?

She tried to sound calm. 'You've had men coming the heavy seduction number before, haven't you?'

'Yes, of course,' said Daisy, although Uncle Bob and Nanny would have been horrified to hear it. They had no idea how times had changed. 'And what did you do about them?' asked Alison, who knew all about Daisy's admirers and knew that Daisy had fallen for none of them. 'You talked them out of it, didn't you? Or laughed them out of it. Or slapped them down if you had to. Well, this is no different. He's just another, trying it on, but this time you act very dignified. Then later you tell me. Then I'll tell Uncle Bob.'

It sounded foolproof. Daisy had no doubt that Richard would accept the dignified rebuke. He wasn't going to lose his self-control. He fancied her, he was not driven by a raging hunger for her. He might call her a prude or an idiot, but more likely he would laugh and shrug because there were plenty more fish in the sea.

'I'm not going to enjoy this,' said Daisy, her palms pressed together, her body rigid. 'This could well be one of the grimmest days of my life ...'

Several times during the hours that followed she remembered saying that, with a prick of guilty surprise because most of the time she was enjoying herself rather too much. It was a beguilingly beautiful day, relaxingly warm, and when she walked back to the cottage Richard was outside, looking under the bonnet of his car.

He was wearing the brown shirt and trousers, and a scarlet kerchief, and he had very broad shoulders. When he was standing his height made them less noticeable, but hunched over the engine he had a boxer's physique. Daisy realised again how strong he must be and that reinforced her resolve to play her part with extreme caution.

She asked, as she reached him, 'Something wrong with the engine? Shall we take my car?'

He grinned at her. 'Just checking. Thanks for the offer, but I don't see myself driving a car with a daisy on the door!'

Her daisy door was much admired. She said, 'It brightens the old girl up.'

'Yes,' he agreed, and straightened, apparently satisfied with the condition of his own engine. 'Did you paint it?'

'No, someone painted it for me.'

'A daisy artist?'

'A design artist,' she said, remembering that hopeful but not very interesting young man and instinctively comparing him with this man. It was unlucky that for sheer personality no one she knew measured up to Richard Lingard.

He looked around. 'No dogs?' and she explained,

'Cooch can be a liability in public, so I took them up to the house.'

'Ready, then?' As ready as she would ever be. She got into the car and it moved away, the engine purring powerfully.

'This is quite a car,' she said.

'I'm glad you approve.' He smiled at her and she dropped her eyes to his hands on the wheel. They were well manicured, but they looked strong and very capable, and she wondered if they could be a farmer's hands.

Golden fields of corn lay either side of them as they left the village along the winding lanes, and she asked, 'How does here compare with the rest of the world?'

'Very well, with the rest of the world I've seen.' Richard had been a wanderer, travelling light with a camera, but he had a home here now and he knew that half the big house and the rolling acres would come to him one day. She asked very casually, 'Have you ever thought of becoming a farmer?'

He laughed at that, and Daisy was sure he hadn't although she wished he had said yes. She had had a sudden faint hope that he might have worked with Keith. The farm could stand two real partners, but like Alison said, that wasn't how Richard would operate. It was just that driving along now in the sunshine, past the cornfields, she was conscious of the strength and vitality of the man beside her as she had never been physically conscious of any other man. The farm could use some of that driving force, if only she could be sure that Richard was not wholly predatory.

She watched his profile. There were no profile pictures of dark Lingards, and it was a bony nose, a real hawklike beak. It made the face look coldly autocratic, although when he turned and smiled the charm flashed warm and mesmeric.

Progress was halted when a herd of milking cows that filled the road ambled round the car, peering in with great

103

lustrous eyes, then moving slowly on. 'I don't think I could stand the country pace,' said Richard.

'If you're in a hurry,' said Daisy with mock severity, 'you've no business in the lanes.' A jet passenger plane flew high overhead in the blue sky and she looked up at it and Richard grinned.

'I take your point.' As the herdsman passed them—black dog at his heels—with a salute of thanks, Richard drew up the car on the grass verge and said, 'I'll get a shot of you here.'

It was just a lane, with meadows stretching to the skyline and the herd of cows ambling away, but Daisy stood where he told her, as she had done the last time in Oak House. Only this time the sun was shining and it was like having holiday snaps taken. She said, 'You think the cows in the background give the right touch for me?'

'You're the one who keeps insisting you're a simple country girl.' That struck a nerve, although she managed to smile. She didn't like being devious, especially when someone was trusting her, and Richard was. There was no aggression in him today, and there wasn't much aggression in Daisy either, and this was not comfortable like most of her relationships were, but exhilarating. If you can be relaxed and exhilarated at the same time.

Richard stopped by an old church in a village that nestled at the bottom of a steep hill. The churchyard was overgrown, grasses waving high between the stones, and he photographed her at the lynchgate, and as they walked down the flagstoned path.

She kept up a patter of local folklore. 'They used to say there were enough witches in this village in the Middle Ages to push a wagon loaded with hay up that hill.'

'That's not very impressive,' said Richard. 'Shouldn't witches worth the name have been able to get a wagon up a hill without putting their shoulders to the wheel?' and Daisy laughed.

'Perhaps they were stronger on pushing power than spell power. That was in Hugo's time, the first dark Lingard.'

'The one who pushed his brother out of the window?'

'You said he didn't,' she reminded him.

'I said it was never proved.'

'Very strong circumstantial evidence, though, wasn't it? This church was here in his day, and you can see which houses were.' Hugo would have known this place, and it was easy to imagine him here—you only had to look at Richard. Only the clothes had to be changed. The Jacobean gentleman, the cosmopolitan of the seventies both had the dark face with the crooked smile.

Daisy fished into her handbag for her spectacles and pointed out the corbels jutting high above. 'They're supposed to be portraits of the workmen who built the church.' Richard took another couple of shots before she took off her spectacles.

'Do you really need those?' he inquired.

'At times. I'm shortsighted.'

'Then why don't you wear them?'

'I only need them for distance, I can see clearly enough close to.' She snapped the case and dropped it into her handbag, then recalled, 'I had them on the first time I looked out of the window and saw you.'

'You weren't wearing them when you came out of the cottage that morning.'

There was no sound but the buzz of insects, bees and gnats. Cars passed on the road and people moved in the cottages, but in the old churchyard the warm air was filled with a gentle humming like a lazy tune. Daisy said, 'I think I wanted you blurred a bit. You were rather a shock.'

'I'm sorry,' he said. 'But not that I came.'

She should say now that she wasn't sorry either, but she had to be, didn't she, when his coming could have such repercussions? Richard stepped back, taking another photograph, and she asked, 'How many of these are you taking?'

'Enough to make a folio for our old age.' He was joking, and she laughed,

'In that case, shall I take one of you?' She wouldn't have dared handle that costly complicated camera, but he said,

'Why? When there's the painting of Hugo. You've seen one dark Lingard, you've seen them all.'

'Do you believe that?'

'No.' The brown hands rested on the thin cheesecloth that covered her shoulders. 'So don't think you've got me taped.'

'Nor you me,' she heard herself answer.

'I'd never make that mistake.' His touch lingered a moment longer while they stood half smiling at each other. Then they continued walking, talking.

In the car Richard turned on the radio and music made a background to their talk, and Daisy deliberately gave herself up to the pleasure of being with a man who kept her bright mind at full stretch. She didn't miss much that day. She seemed to be seeing more and hearing more, laughing more, arguing more.

As they waited at a traffic light she glanced into the window of an antique shop and saw a large Chinese lion in green porcelain, wide mouth stretched in a grotesque grin. 'There's Cooch,' she said. 'Isn't he handsome?' and it did have a vague resemblance to a pekingese dog.

But she was unprepared for Richard's turning down a side street, finding a parking spot, leaving her there and returning within minutes, having bought the lion.

It must have cost a great deal of money, and when he handed it to her she stammered, 'However much did you pay for this?'

'Don't be so mercenary!' he grinned, but in the circumstances she hadn't wanted him spending anything on her, and she protested, distressed,

'You shouldn't have done it.'

106

'Why not? He's an ugly little guy, but he's no uglier than Cooch.'

Actually she liked it immensely, but she went on biting her lip, looking bothered, and he said, 'Don't be so bloody independent.'

'I'm sorry, but I am independent.'

'Fair enough, but don't be neurotic about it.' He didn't know why she couldn't accept a gift like this without feeling guilty.

'I'll be right back,' she said frantically, and went rushing off. She had to get something for him so that at least he couldn't accuse her of being a gold-digger today. She only had a few pounds on her, but she had a cheque book and a bank card. She went into the same antique shop, which was open for tourist trade, and once in there couldn't imagine what on earth she could buy. She was almost sure Richard would follow her, and the shop had a good quota of strollers and she found herself looking wildly around.

She had no idea what his tastes were. The first day he came to Oak House he had looked at the furniture and the paintings very shrewdly, but that could have been natural interest. Or even then he could have been wondering what Uncle Bob was worth.

Daisy blocked that from her mind. She must buy something quickly, so she picked up a fortune-teller's crystal ball, on a tiny crystal stand, upended the stand and read the price, and decided that would do.

She was signing the cheque when she saw Richard, and she said to the girl with the long limp hair who was serving her, 'Would you wrap it up quickly, please, because I've bought it for the man who's just coming through the door, and I don't want him to see it.'

The girl's eyes followed directions and brightened like little lamps turned on. She straightened her stooping shoulders and said, 'He's just bought the Chinese lion,' as though that made him a bosom friend, although Daisy knew he would have had the same effect if this had been the first time he had walked in here. He was getting sizing-up looks from several women in his progress from the door to Daisy.

When he reached her he asked, 'What are you doing?'

'Coming,' she said. The assistant gave her her parcel, eyes fixed on Richard, so that Daisy felt quite pleased by an admiring look from a middle-aged male, who remarked to his wife in a strong American accent as she passed,

'Now that's what I call a real English rose, Mother.'

'Come on, English Daisy,' said Richard.

'Ha!' said Daisy. 'The way that assistant looked at you I'll bet she let you have the lion at cost.'

'She might have done if I'd had time to bargain. What have you bought?'

'Wait,' she said.

In the car she handed him the bag. 'For you,' she said, and he took out the heavy crystal ball.

'Thank you,' he said, with a touch of irony because Daisy was so obviously anxious not to be in his debt. This hadn't cost nearly as much as the lion, but her gesture had not been simple generosity. He looked at her flushed and pretty face and asked, 'Can you read the future?'

'No.' A small shiver went up her spine, and he said at once,

'It frightens you?' What she knew of her immediate future she didn't like much. She said quietly,

'Shouldn't it frighten everyone, these days?' and Richard leaned back in the car seat, eyeing her thoughtfully. Then he nodded.

'There's something in that. So we'll just take today.' He put the crystal ball in the glove compartment. 'Let's eat,' he said.

They joined the tourists, walking through the crowds, ending in a restaurant that Daisy knew was reputed for its cuisine and its prices. She would have been happier with somewhere less pricey like one of the pubs they had passed, or one of the colourful cheaper little cafés around the town. But when Richard said, 'Here, I think,' he wasn't asking for her opinion.

They hadn't booked and the dining room was almost full, but they got a good table and good service, neither of which seemed to surprise Richard, and Daisy realised he was used to that. He expected the best, which meant he probably lived to the limits of his earnings. The car suggested that too, but then he had no responsibilities, so why shouldn't he?

They chose wine, and food: whitebait, steak and salad; and Daisy asked, 'Are you interested in food?'

'I have the usual appetites.'

'I'm sure you have.' They smiled at each other and he said,

'Food isn't one of my obsessions.'

'What are your obsessions?' Power, he had once said, making a joke of it, but he was a powerful man. Just sitting here, eating a civilised meal, with him smiling at her and talking softly, Daisy was still conscious of his steely strength.

'I'll tell you one day,' he said, and predictably, 'What about yours?'

She answered honestly, 'Oak House, I think.'

'The past. Is that why you don't want to look into the future?'

'Maybe,' she said, 'I don't see much future for it.' She would have given a great deal for a sign of reassurance, but all he said was,

'Don't you?' as though he didn't see much either. But it was a good lunch and Richard was stimulating company.

She caught the eye of a man at one of the other tables by accident, smiling instinctively in answer to his smile as she turned away, but knowing that he was still watching them. He was a stranger to Daisy, florid and tweedily dressed, and after a moment Richard asked, 'What is it?'

She looked again at their fellow diner. 'Isn't he trying to attract our attention?'

As Richard turned from profile to full face the man smiled once more. It was Richard he knew, and he leaned forward with what seemed to be happy expectancy, but all he got was a curt unsmiling nod. Daisy felt his embarrassment. She had never seen a blunter brush-off, and she was sorry for the man, who had been smiling.

'Why did you do that?' she demanded. 'Who is he?'

'A bore,' drawled Richard. 'If he'd come over we'd never have got rid of him.'

'You didn't have to look at him as though he was less than the dust!'

'Do you want to meet him? His obsession is sewerage.'

'No, but——'

'So eat up your pudding, as Nanny would say.'

Daisy finished her fruit compote rather faster than she might have done, and she wasn't sorry to get out of the dining room. She glanced apologetically at the snubbed sewerage expert as she headed for the door, and he smiled at her without apparent rancour. Richard didn't give him a second look.

They meandered through the Cotswold countryside. They sat on a river bank. It was very easy to like Richard when the rakish charm was masking the arrogance, because Daisy always had been a little in love with the dark Lingards. She had measured the real-life admirers against them for excitement, but now there was a living dark Lingard wanting her, and she was finding his nearness delightfully disturbing. When he touched her it registered on a nerve length she had never felt before, so that her skin tingled at the lightest contact.

During that day the truce was real, and before they turned for home Daisy was asking herself why it shouldn't go on. Richard wanted her, but more important he *liked* her. Sometimes today they had talked about quite serious things, so why shouldn't they discuss Uncle Ben's decision about the farm? She and Alison had taken it for granted that Richard would want everything sold up, but Richard was a Lingard, and the dark Lingards had all kept the place going.

'When are you seeing Michael Langley again?' Richard asked as they turned into the drive.

She shrugged, 'I don't know.'

'Good.' Although she hadn't said she wasn't seeing Michael again she knew that she wouldn't, and she hoped that Anne, his sister who worked with her, wouldn't mind. Her Mini was where she had left it, and Richard turned his car alongside.

Then he sat with a hand on the wheel, another along the back of the seat behind her, looking at her with open admiration, telling her, 'I still can't understand how the men you go around with keep their hands off you,' and she enjoyed a female moment of pure tease.

'I never said they did. I didn't say I was untouched, just uncommitted.'

'Then they can't have been very adept in their lovemaking.' He was teasing her now, eyes gleaming with laughter, and Daisy thought wryly that he probably had few complaints about his technique, he was so obviously experienced. He had been making love to her all day, by word and look and casual touch, and as she moved to open the car door he said, 'Do we share a cup of coffee?'

'There's the rest of the wine. I recorked it.'

'You are a careful girl!'

'Did you expect me to drink it?' She might ask him about the farm now, or even tell him what Alison had overheard. Why shouldn't he and Keith work out something together? She offered, 'Tinned tomato soup and toast?'

'One of my favourite meals.'

She put the Chinese lion on the dresser, then went into

111

the kitchen and Richard went to her bookcase, where he would find a wide range of old and new. He took out a volume and sat down. If he looked up he would see her at the stove through the kitchen door, and she looked across at him as she heated the soup.

She wondered what book he had taken out, and as the first sluggish bubble reached the surface of the soup she began to stir, releasing a small scalding gusher on to her bare arm. She yelped with pain, dropping the spoon in the soup, and Richard jumped up.

'How can it do that when it's still nearly cold?' she gibbered. He turned on the tap and held her arm under it until the sting of the scald subsided. He had also taken off the soup, and when she looked back at the stove he didn't release her.

'Come and sit down,' he said.

Daisy was slightly shaky and she went meekly. She knew he was going to kiss her, and the gentle pressure of his lips and his arms around her was comforting. She snuggled against him on the sofa, feeling a rising tide of excitement as the muscles in his arms tensed and hardened, crushing her closer, and his mouth was over her mouth as she tried to mumble, 'No.'

'Yes,' he said, still kissing her.

She almost struggled, but somehow her lips parted and her bones were melting, her hands were locked behind his head, and she kissed him and it was the first time she had kissed or been kissed. All the others were nothing.

She felt her blouse slip from her shoulder, the light trailing pressure of lips and fingers releasing the undiscovered instincts of her body. She responded ardently but blindly, attuned to nothing but the nearness of this man. This was a hunger she hadn't known, a racing, divine madness that would have carried her by storm to the heights or the depths.

Her eyes were tight closed, but Woo's barking reached

112

her, and she looked into Richard's face and he said, 'They're coming.'

Alison was coming, and Daisy struggled upright, feeling as though she had been flung out of a chairoplane on hard unmoving earth, her head still whirling, shaken out of her wits. She clutched at her blouse, jerking it back over her shoulders, cringing away from him. 'Would you—go, please?' Her voice cracked. She was aghast at herself. She would have let Richard make love to her. She had responded to every caress, lost her head completely.

'Why?' he said. He was cool enough. The interruption would be unwelcome, but he had never been out of control, and shame and confusion scalded her so that she was a burning blush from head to toe. She jumped up and she wasn't even steady on her feet.

'Because I'm asking you,' she almost shrieked. 'Get out, will you?'

'No.'

'Then I will.' She had to get away from where he was sitting so calm and quiet, and she flung open the door and ran past Alison, the dogs following her. Running from herself, not from Richard, from the girl who had woken at a kiss, but from the wrong man at the wrong time.

CHAPTER SIX

DAISY heard Alison calling her, but right now she couldn't
face anyone and she went on running, both dogs with her,
Woo happily convinced this was a game, a race for the fun
of it, Cooch snorting like a small warhorse. She ran through
the dusk, blundering off the track among the trees in a state
of dazed disbelief.

Alison was still calling, 'Daisy, wait for me!' and Daisy
leaned against a beech tree, clapping cold hands to her forehead, struggling to pull herself together. If only her head
would stop whirling it would be all right.

She had just reacted like a ravished maiden in a Victorian melodrama. Richard must have thought she had gone
raving mad, and she must have frightened Alison, who was
now shouting frantically, 'Daisy, where *are* you? Please
Daisy, *wait*!'

Two hysterical women, thought Daisy, and a pekingese
keening like a banshee. We'll have all the family down here,
probably all the village, if we don't shut up. She called, 'I'm
here!' Alison would have heard Cooch anyway and Daisy
was saying, 'It's all right, hush, it's all right,' to the dog as
Alison rounded the beech tree and croaked,

'Daisy, are you all right?'

'Yes,' said Daisy.

Alison's face was white in the shadows and she clutched
Daisy to her. 'What happened?' she demanded.

'Nothing,' said Daisy. 'A little necking, that's all.'

Alison fell back a step in astonishment. 'You screamed
"Get out!" at him. You *ran*.'

114

'I know.' Daisy had made such a spectacle of herself, and she couldn't start to explain.

'You nearly knocked me over,' Alison squealed. 'And you didn't even see Uncle Bob.'

'Was he there?'

'He wanted to see Richard, about the will, I suppose, so he said he'd walk down with me.' She stared hard at Daisy, then said slowly, 'If you're really all right it couldn't have been better. I suppose you heard Woo barking?'

'Yes.'

'I never knew you were that good an actress.' Alison was awed. 'You can imagine how Uncle Bob reacted. You had me scared. I just stood there gawping and Uncle Bob was raging, "What's going on here?" Didn't you hear him?'

Daisy had heard nothing. She had just run, head down. She shook her head now and asked, 'What did Richard say?'

'He said, "Well, well".' As Alison repeated that it struck her as odd. 'Funny thing to say,' she commented.

'Just that?' said Daisy.

'That was when I got my breath back and started calling you. What do you think we ought to do now? I think we should go up to the house.'

Daisy certainly couldn't face returning to the cottage where Uncle Bob might still be raging. She didn't want to see Richard again tonight. She would be keeping out of his way as much as possible in future. She groaned, 'Oh, I have made such a fool of myself, shrieking like something out of *East Lynne*.'

'Perhaps you did overplay it.' Alison had been shocked and scared when she heard Daisy shout, 'Get out, will you?' and when Daisy rushed from the cottage it hadn't looked like acting. But Daisy said it was and she wasn't hurt and Alison tried to make her smile. 'But Uncle Bob's out of *East Lynne* himself, really, isn't he? With any luck he'll tell Richard never to darken his doors again.'

115

'It isn't funny.' Daisy turned towards Oak House. 'I feel sick about it.'

Alison walked beside her. Cooch was still muttering, his fur stiff, his eyes rolling, an angry dog because his mistress was distressed.

'I know,' said Alison. 'But you don't have to do anything else now Uncle Bob's seen for himself. You can just say you don't want to talk about it.'

Daisy did not want to talk. She went into the house with Alison, and up to Alison and Keith's room. Keith and Nanny were probably in the kitchen and Nanny would want to know all about Daisy's outing today with Richard. After a while Alison would go down, and say that Daisy thought she might have a touch of 'flu and was staying the night. Daisy would sleep in the guest room and preserve a belated dignified silence about Richard's outrageous behaviour.

'I'm not pretending,' said Daisy, lying on Alison's bed. 'I've got a splitting headache. All I want to do is go to sleep and try to forget it.'

'You do that,' Alison soothed her. 'Nanny will be up, of course, as soon as I say you're not feeling well.'

'I'll go into the guest room in a few minutes. Tell her I'm asleep.' Daisy closed her eyes. 'Do you think Uncle Bob will tell her anything?'

Alison couldn't say. Things had taken a more dramatic turn than they'd anticipated. Alison had rehearsed how she would tell Uncle Bob that Richard was a womaniser, who saw Daisy as fair prey. But she hadn't expected Daisy to get into such a state, and she was still worried about what must have happened to upset Daisy so much.

They both tried to talk about something else. Alison had been visiting this afternoon, and she gave Daisy every bit of news she had gleaned, spreading it out, right down to a detailed description of a new carpet, while Daisy pretended to be immensely interested.

But when the door opened and Nanny walked in the sisters jumped guiltily, as though they were ten years younger and had been up to mischief. And when Nanny said, 'There you are, the master wants you,' Daisy gulped and stammered,

'W-who?'

'You,' said Nanny. 'What've you been doing?'

'I can't——' Daisy started to protest, but Alison said,

'I'll come with you. Let's get it over with.'

Nanny hadn't really thought that Daisy had done anything to displease Robert Lingard, although he had looked very serious when he'd come in just now, asking if they'd seen Daisy and Alison. But the sisters' attitude was surprising her and she asked sharply, 'What's the matter?'

'Nothing,' Daisy said hurriedly. 'Where is he?'

'In the study. What does he want you for?' Nanny had a quick awareness of trouble in the family, and there had been uneasy currents lately. She liked Richard very much, but she could see how things were going and she prayed nightly that everything would turn out right in the end. By right she meant Richard's acceptance, all the family—including Richard—united.

Neither Daisy nor Alison answered her. They went quickly, leaving her smoothing down the bed coverlet that Daisy had rumpled. Just as she helped Alison paint the walls Nanny tidied the house as she went, as though bright colours and order in Oak House would keep out the chaos of the outside world. But lately there had been strained faces and trouble in the air.

As Daisy and Alison went downstairs Daisy said, 'I'm not going to make a big production of this.'

'You already have,' Alison pointed out, and Daisy flinched from that memory, insisting,

'Well, I'm going to play it down now.'

'Let's see what's happening,' said Alison. Whatever Daisy said now Uncle Bob had heard and seen her, running

117

away from Richard. He would form his own conclusions that Richard was a promiscuous opportunist.

But Richard was in the study too. Uncle Bob sat at the desk, Richard stood by the window, and when the girls walked in Uncle Bob said, 'Come and sit down, Daisy-girl.'

She couldn't look at Richard, as he brought a chair forward. She sat down, scarlet-cheeked and eyes downcast, and Richard said, 'Alison, would you mind?'

'Mind what?' asked Alison.

'Out,' he said, then smiled, 'Please.'

Uncle Bob said nothing, so it seemed that Richard was giving the orders. Protests trembled on Alison's lips, but she backed out of the room, through the door that Richard held open for her, looking daggers at him. He closed the door, then turned to Daisy and inquired solicitously, 'How's the arm?'

'What?' Her brow furrowed.

'Your arm. You splashed it with hot soup.'

She had forgotten, and there was nothing to show but a faint reddening of the skin that was tender when she touched it. Richard's concern was highly suspicious, his expression wasn't matching his voice.

He was facing Daisy, with his back to Uncle Bob, as he said gently, 'I'm sorry I frightened you. I lost my head when I took you in my arms, but it won't happen again.' She was sure it wouldn't. His voice was warm and hesitant, but his eyes were keen as a dueller's. 'I would never have hurt you,' he said. 'I guess you know that I've far too much respect for you.

'Respect, and love,' he added fervently, while she gasped for breath. 'It was love at first sight from that first morning, and every day I've known you since it has grown deeper. You are the sweetest girl I've ever met, the gentlest and the kindest, and I should be the happiest man in the world if I thought there was a chance that one day you would become my wife.'

118

There was no answer to that. It was unmitigated clap-trap, all for Uncle Bob's benefit, and Daisy wanted to scream, 'Stop it!'

'My intentions,' said Richard, his voice shaking—with laughter, although Uncle Bob wasn't to know that, 'are entirely honourable. Your unworldliness, your artlessness, have been an inspiration to me, Daisy. In you I think I've found my ideal woman.'

'You're too flattering,' she said faintly.

'Can I hope——?' He leaned towards her as though he would have touched her, and that was too much.

'No,' she said. 'Thank you, but no.' Richard sighed deeply and Uncle Bob said,

'Don't be too hasty. You don't have to make up your mind like that. Think about it.'

About marrying Richard? That wasn't a genuine proposal. Even if it had been Daisy would have turned it down, but it was pure mickey-taking, making a fool of her with every word. Sweet and gentle and artless and unworldly were the absolute opposite to what he really thought about about her.

Uncle Bob got up and came round to put a hand on Daisy's shoulder. 'Pretty girls can make men fall in love with them without realising what they're doing,' he said. 'Remember that, child.' Then he gave Richard an encouraging nod and left them, cumbersomely tactful, Uncle Bob the matchmaker, leaving Daisy croaking and Richard chuckling.

'There's one worry he needn't have,' said Richard. 'There's one pretty girl who knows exactly what she's doing.'

Daisy got her voice from somewhere, shrill and shaking. 'He can't believe what you've been saying!'

'If he believes in you he'll believe anything.' He smiled the crooked smile, then sat on the edge of the desk, grinning down at her. 'Are you taking up my offer?'

119

'Marry you?' She flung back her head and tried to sound as mocking as he did. 'You've probably got a wife and family already.' As she said that she realised how little they did know about him when it came down to brass tacks. 'All I know for sure about you is that you are a liar,' she snapped.

'And you,' he said cheerfully, 'are a conniving little witch. You and that sister of yours set me up, didn't you?'

He knew they had, and she glared at him, demanding, 'Why don't you go back to wherever you came from and leave us alone?'

'No chance.' He looked like a man who was enjoying himself. 'I'm getting more laughs here than I've had in years.'

Daisy got up to get out, and he gave her a mocking bow. 'Your obedient humble servant, ma'am.'

'Oh, shut up!' she snapped.

'Make up your mind what period you're living in, the past or the present.' She probably wouldn't have replied to that, but as he went straight on she had no chance. 'But you do know, don't you?' he said. 'That was some performance. Some timing, dead on cue. And old Robert still believes you're the original shrinking violet.'

She was nearer Uncle Bob's idea of her than Richard's. She was a modern girl, but she had unsophisticated ideals of love and loyalty—that, once given, both should last a lifetime. If she had been as blasé as Richard imagined she wouldn't have gone to pieces just now. That hadn't been a performance, dead on cue. That had been black panic, and by making such a scene she had played right into his hands. He had fooled Uncle Bob completely, taking the blame for 'frightening' Daisy by pretending he'd lost his head because he was desperately in love with her.

Honourable intentions indeed! She said raggedly, 'What will you do if I call your bluff and say all right, I'll marry you?'

120

'No danger.' He was a man who knew how to play a rough game, and there was menace in the hard eyes and the softly spoken words. 'Even if you can't read the crystal ball you're sharp enough to know it wouldn't pay you to put your future into my hands.'

Her eyes slid away from him. She couldn't look at him, but she had to say, 'You've no right here. Not like this, pushing Keith out.'

He was still baiting her, laughing at her. The tiny muscle moved in his cheek. 'More right than you, Daisy Penrose, blood being thicker than water. And didn't you tell me that the dark Lingards were all master here, each in his own time?'

'Not yet,' she muttered.

'I can wait.' If he meant until Uncle Bob died that could be another ten years or more, but Robert Lingard was an old man and as his strength failed Richard's hold could strengthen.

'When I'm master,' said Richard, 'I'll let you know if I need a mistress.'

Daisy's cheeks and eyes burned. 'You'd be lucky,' she said with blistering scorn.

'No? You're probably right. You've got a delectable body, but your mind's a shade too calculating. So we'll just stay good neighbours and I'll let you keep the cottage.'

'I'm not going back to the cottage while you're in the barn,' she burst out impulsively, and he tutted at her like Nanny.

'What's the fuss? Where's the worry? I respect you. I worship you from afar—and the farther the better. You could do a striptease by moonlight without turning me on —I don't make the same mistake twice.'

The door opened and Alison's worried face peered at them. 'Come in,' said Richard.

'All right, Daisy?' asked Alison.

'If you mean still virginal,' drawled Richard, 'that's her

121

story and old Robert believes it. I'll leave you two to compare notes. By the way, was Keith in on this?'

'On what?' stammered Alison.

'No,' said Daisy.

'I'm inclined to believe you,' said Richard.

Alison stared at the door as he closed it behind him. She had waited, sitting on the stairs, peering through the banisters, and seen Uncle Bob come out of the study smiling. That flabbergasted Alison, and after another couple of minutes she could contain herself no longer, she had to find out what was going on. 'Why did Uncle Bob leave you two alone?' she asked, and Daisy moved restlessly up and down the room, pacing the old red Turkish carpet, her voice as quick and jerky as her movements.

'Because Richard's intentions are honourable. That's what he told Uncle Bob, and Uncle Bob was quite won over. It seems that Richard is madly in love with me, but he has far too much respect for my maidenly modesty to have gone farther than an ardent embrace, and of course he wants to marry me.'

Alison was watching Daisy like someone following a tennis match, head now this way, now that, very much as Cooch was watching her. Then she latched on to the last two words. '*Marry* you? Did he ask you to marry him?'

Daisy laughed weakly. 'He didn't *mean* it.' She had expected Alison to recognise her sarcasm, but here was Alison wondering if Richard and Daisy might marry and the four of them settle down on the farm together. 'It was all to impress Uncle Bob,' Daisy explained. 'For goodness' sake, you heard him just now. Did he sound in love with me?'

Alison bit her lip, shaking her head regretfully.

'You should have heard him before you came in,' said Daisy. 'He knows we set him up, you and me. A pair of conniving witches is what we are.' She straightened the heavy black and gilt ink and pen stand that was a little awry on the desk, and moved the pewter ashtray the merest fraction. 'He even thinks I pretended to scald myself when I was heating up some soup so that he'd put his arms around me and things would get passionate on cue for you to arrive with Uncle Bob.'

'Did you?' Alison asked automatically, and Daisy said,

'Of course not. I didn't know Uncle Bob was coming, did I?'

The study was a cluttered room. It was the office where all the paperwork for the farm was done, and the furniture was old and massive. The chair behind the desk was a swivel armchair and Daisy gave it a full spin before she said, 'Anyhow, that little plan didn't work. Uncle Bob thinks I led Richard on without realising it, and I'm not to be too hasty turning him down, I'm to think about it, because wouldn't it be super if Richard married me?'

While anger was still coursing through her veins—remembering the things Richard had just said to her—she couldn't accept defeat. Alison sat down, in the chair Richard had placed for Daisy, and asked pleadingly, because it was the only way out that she could see, 'Are you sure it wouldn't work?'

'I'm sure,' said Daisy harshly, 'that Richard had Uncle Bob believing him. Of course he doesn't want to marry me —nor do I want to marry him, thank you very much—but he is a good con-man, I can tell you that.'

She sat down in the swivel chair, facing Alison. 'And that's all I can tell you for sure about him,' she said. 'Have you ever stopped to think how much we're taking Richard on trust? He walks in one Sunday morning and announces that he's Andrew's grandson, without producing one single scrap of real evidence.'

'But of course he's——' Alison began. She paused, catching her breath. 'I mean, the way he looks ...'

'Which could be coincidence.' Daisy spoke slowly, but her mind was darting on suspicions that must have been subconsciously stored, as she sat back in the big chair

123

stating the case against the man who could be an impostor. 'He'd seen the pictures, looking like him, and read the article before he came here. He says his name's Lingard, but it could be Smith for all we know, and he went to the Three Feathers first—that's where he spent Saturday night, where any of the old regulars might have told him about Andrew who went off to America and hasn't been heard of for forty years.'

'I suppose they could have done,' Alison agreed. Richard had been so convincing, with such self-assurance, that she had never questioned anything he had told them, but now Daisy was raising exciting doubts, reminding her.

'Nobody wanted proof of identity. He was welcomed with open arms and told he could use this as his home, free board, free lodging. All he had to do was say that Andrew was dead and Andrew's son was dead and there were no other relations. And his parents hadn't married, so he didn't want any publicity about another dark Lingard turning up.'

Pieces seemed to be slotting into a pattern. Daisy was astonishing herself by her perspicacity. 'You remember how angry he was when I said it would make a follow-up story? He threatened to walk out, although I thought then that he didn't seem like a man who'd worry that much about being illegitimate.'

Alison remembered and Daisy was right. All they knew about Richard was what he had told them, and why should they accept that as the whole truth?

'He's been here over two months,' Daisy was saying, 'and he's never accepted any invitations. He hasn't even been out with Keith, has he? He doesn't meet anyone unless they come here, unless he's working or seeing business contacts, and he's never brought anyone to meet us. There's a sort of—void around him. We don't even know for sure where he goes, the days and nights he isn't here.'

'He never makes phone calls from the house that I've heard of, nor had anyone call him,' Alison recalled excitedly. 'I don't know about mail. I wonder if he gets any mail—he's never had any at the house.'

'I've never seen any.' They were leaning towards each other now, eager and apprehensive, hardly daring to believe what this might mean. 'And there was this man where we had lunch today who recognised him, and Richard cut him dead. He didn't even speak to him as we went out.'

'Because he knows Richard by another name?' Alison suggested gleefully. 'Or at any rate something that Richard didn't want you to hear?'

'And another thing,' said Daisy. 'He's shown us photographs he's taken, but we've never seen any published, have we? You'd think he'd have produced a magazine or something. But if they don't say "Richard Lingard" he'd have some explaining to do. And we don't *know* he's Richard Lingard. He looks like the old pictures, but he could have called here out of curiosity and found a cushy billet. So cushy that Uncle Bob is ready to make over half the farm to him.'

Some of Alison's elation ebbed. 'He'd be named in the will. He must be Richard Lingard. It wouldn't be legal if it wasn't his name.'

'He could always tell Uncle Bob he was registered in his mother's name—he said Uncle Bob would believe anything. But whether he's a Lingard or not, we've only seen the tip of the iceberg.'

Daisy had always felt Richard was hiding more than he was telling, but it said a great deal for his powerful personality that nobody here had questioned him searchingly about anything. He looked like a dark Lingard, and he acted as you would expect one to act. But he had been knocking around for thirty odd years before he'd turned up at Oak House Farm and it might be illuminating to know what he had been doing, apart from the colourful anecdotes with which he entertained them.

'It shouldn't be hard to find out,' said Daisy, 'for a start

125

we could say, "How do we know you're who you say you are?"'

'Now?' asked Alison, not very enthusiastically.

'Not tonight,' said Daisy. 'Not me. I've had enough for one day.' She wasn't equal to another clash with Richard just yet. She said, 'I think I will stay in the guest room, and I think I'll go up now.'

Alison was all for that. Daisy had been through an ordeal for which Alison felt responsible. As the older married sister she had always 'babied' Daisy a little, and now she wanted to tuck her up with a hot drink, and tell her that a good night's sleep was what she needed.

But Daisy knew that. She looked tired, but determined, and steadier than Alison felt. 'I don't advise you to say anything to him either,' she told Alison. 'He's angry with both of us, and if he is Richard Lingard, and you ask to see his passport tonight, it will be the last straw and he'll blast you.'

Alison had a terrifying vision of Richard's anger unleashed, and all this was wishful thinking; he probably was Andrew's grandson. She said sadly, 'You do think he's a Lingard, don't you?'

Daisy opened the door and looked out, relieved to find the coast clear. 'I know he's hiding something,' she said, 'and tomorrow we'll do some detective work.'

She got upstairs to the guest room without meeting anyone, and turned on a bar of the electric fire, because although it was a warm evening she had the shivers. She took off her shoes and sat on the rug in front of the fire, rubbing her feet.

Downstairs Alison might be facing Richard, although Daisy felt it more likely that she was dodging him. She would tell whoever asked that Daisy wasn't feeling too good and was staying here for the night, and Daisy had better hurry into bed because that would almost certainly bring Nanny up.

126

She crept barefoot to the bathroom, not daring to put on a light because Richard walked around this house as freely as anybody, and with her luck today she could walk straight into him, especially as Cooch was snuffling along at her heels.

She couldn't face Richard again tonight. After work tomorrow, yes, and then she would ask him a few things. He had made Uncle Bob believe he wanted to marry her. If he was that interested in her she was surely entitled to be interested in him, and wonder why he had never brought anyone home to meet his family.

While they were on families, maybe he did have a wife somewhere. If he was a married man playing around that would blacken him irrevocably in Uncle Bob's eyes, and Daisy felt tearing revulsion, fierce as jealousy. If not a wife of course there would be women, and she found she was still scowling about that, as she scurried back into the guest room where Alison was waiting with hot milk, three arrowroot biscuits, and a nightdress.

'Richard's in with Uncle Bob,' said Alison straightaway. 'What shall I tell Keith? He and Nanny are driving me crazy, wanting to know what's going on.'

'Tell them Richard and I have had a blazing row,' said Daisy. 'That shouldn't surprise them, and it's the truth.'

'Yes,' Alison agreed, 'I'd better leave it at that. Keith wouldn't approve at all of what we did.'

That wasn't news to Daisy. Keith bitterly resented losing what he had always considered his birthright, but he would have been very uptight about their scheming. Daisy said, with enforced lightness, 'Richard's only blaming you and me. He knows Keith's a gentleman.'

'What's wrong with being a gentleman?' Alison was quickly on the defensive, and Daisy said just as quickly,

'Nothing at all, it's a pity Richard isn't.' That would have narrowed the odds and given Keith a better chance, but Richard played to win.

127

She drank her milk, but found she couldn't swallow the biscuits. She turned out the fire and the light and got into the big bed with its shiny mahogany head and foot boards, plumped up the pillows behind her and lay there, her eyes growing accustomed to the dark.

She had slept in here before, the first time as a child with measles when Nanny had nursed her. She knew all the furniture as well as her own cottage, as well as the other rooms in this house. But tonight there was something disturbing about being here, because Richard had been the last guest in this guest room.

As she'd brushed her hair, in front of the swinging mirror on top of the chest of drawers, she had remembered that the last man's face reflected there was Richard's. For no real reason she'd put down the hairbrush, and moved away from the mirror to finish undressing and get into Alison's nightdress. She drank her milk by the fire, then climbed into bed.

Cooch slept on the rug beside the bed, snoring in his sleep as he always did, and as the room became clearer for Daisy she couldn't banish Richard from it. A dark man in the shadows, a big man moving quietly. She found she was sitting rigidly upright and made herself lie down and stretch slowly, arms and legs, then as slowly relax, loosening the tense muscles. Three hundred years ago they had believed in demon lovers, but whoever Richard was he was very human. It was a man she couldn't get out of her mind, and it was the first time any man had kept her from sleep.

When she did sleep he invaded her dreams. She was walking with him somewhere the wind blew, over high fields or on clifftops. Walking with the wind blowing all around. He was masked, although she knew it was Richard, and each time she stretched out a hand she touched the mask. But each time she drew back, and the walking became harder, her feet heavier. At last he went ahead into the gale, and she couldn't follow him. She was chained down, bogged in, struggling and helpless.

She woke gasping, with a dead weight across her feet, and that was that aspect of the dream explained. Cooch was asleep on her feet, and as she dragged them from under he grumbled and padded to an unoccupied spot of the bed.

If the dog hadn't jumped on the bed Daisy wondered if she would have kept pace with the dream, even taken off the mask at last. But she hadn't been eager about the unmasking. Maybe she was scared what she was going to learn, although surely the worse the better for Alison and Keith.

He *was* Richard Lingard. She was almost sure of that in spite of everything, and he was angry with her. Good and mad because he thought they had tried to get him into Uncle Bob's bad books. They had, of course, but not as cunningly as he imagined. Anyhow, he had talked his way out of it.

Lying there in the darkness, cosy and comfortable, she wasn't angry any more. Her indignation had faded into wry admiration as her sense of humour surfaced again. Richard was a wretch, he had made a complete idiot of her, but he was a very resourceful wretch; and maybe after a night's sleep he wouldn't be so angry either.

She would say, 'How do we know you're who you say you are?' But he *was* a dark Lingard, and she might also say, 'I'm sorry about last night. I was going to let Uncle Bob know you'd made a pass at me, and he is very strait-laced and I did hope it would put him off you, because I don't think it's fair the way Keith is in second place now. But I didn't know he was going to walk down to the cottage with Alison, and it wasn't a performance. The soup splashing was an accident, and I lost my head because——'

Lying here, drowsy and warm, she felt she could explain the unexpected turmoil of emotion that had made her responsive in his arms, how the barking of the dog had shattered her. That nothing she did in the cottage last even-

129

ing had been done in cool deliberation.

But when she woke next morning she was less confident —a great deal less. What it came down to was that Richard was the most attractive man she had ever met, and not only had her body melted at his touch but so had her mind, leaving her daft as a brush, and she couldn't see herself admitting that in cold blood.

Nanny and Alison were in the kitchen when Daisy came down, and Woo, who had slept by the embers of the fire, came bounding to greet her. Cooch followed her, bleary-eyed, and Nanny asked, 'How's your health and temper this morning?'

'Fine,' said Daisy.

'Because we can do without the tantrums,' said Nanny severely.

Alison, who was frying bacon, sausages and tomatoes, at the stove, looked across at Daisy, ruefully amused. The conflict between Daisy and Richard hardly came into the tantrum category.

'Have a cup of tea,' said Alison. If Nanny hadn't been here they would have continued their conversation of last night, because this was the day the detective work started, and Alison was hoping that Daisy would do it. She had always believed she was stronger than Daisy, but she was leaning on Daisy now. When Daisy had warned her last night not to anger Richard any more, she had felt cold perspiration at the thought of it. She was no match for him herself, but she had a desperate hope that Daisy might be.

Daisy was pouring tea when Uncle Bob arrived. He was usually silent in the mornings, eating his breakfast and reading his newspaper with only the odd grunt. But this morning he beamed on them all, with a special twinkle for Daisy, and said, 'I've got something for you, Daisy-girl.' He dug into his pocket and brought out a letter, which Daisy accepted gingerly.

Uncle Bob sat down and informed them, 'Richard will

be away till the weekend,' and thanked Nanny, who put a plate of food in front of him.

As Daisy tore open the envelope Alison held her breath. It was a short note. 'Daisy—I won't see you again until the weekend. Work, you understand. Think of me. I shall think of you. R.'

Silently Daisy handed Alison the sheet of paper, torn from the memo pad in the study, and Alison breathed again. He wasn't threatening anything, unless you read a threat between the lines. Uncle Bob would take it for a respectful billet-doux, but he didn't know what Richard really thought of Daisy.

'Away for the whole week,' said Alison tartly. 'He'll be missed.'

'Did he leave a phone number?' Daisy asked Uncle Bob, who told her,

'He said he'd be moving around.'

'He does a lot of that, doesn't he?' Alison was smiling, but her voice was shaking. 'He must make a lot of friends, although we've never met any of them. And Daisy and I were saying only last night that no one has ever asked for any proof at all that he's who he says he is.' She stopped there, expecting an outburst from Uncle Bob, but he only said mildly,

'What makes you think nobody has?'

'Have you?' asked Daisy eagerly.

'Oh yes.' He picked up his knife and fork and waded into his breakfast, closing the subject so that it was impossible to ask what proof had been given. Especially as he had looked reproachfully at Alison. She wasn't doing Keith any good sniping at Richard. They would have to have a very solid case against him before Uncle Bob would even listen.

When she got back from work that evening Daisy had planned her first, obvious move—to get into the barn. She was not convinced that Uncle Bob had asked for proof of identity, and it was possible there would be papers in the

131

barn, and they had to start somewhere.

She wasn't too hopeful because Richard had left a key at the farm, so they were unlikely to find the story of his life lying around. But she would have settled for a handkerchief with the wrong initials, or the name of his agent, or an address anywhere else in the world.

With a key she felt less like a snooper, although Alison hovering behind her was muttering, 'Wouldn't it be awful if he came back and caught us? What would we say we were doing?'

'There'd be no need to explain,' said Daisy wryly. 'He'd know what we were doing. I expect he expects it.' She would not have been surprised to find another note addressed to 'Daisy' in here, even briefer than the last and more to the point. Something like, 'You'll be lucky.'

But there was no note. There was nothing. Planning permission hadn't come through yet for the real renovations, and there were the essentials for Spartan living, and no more. No papers, no briefcase. He travelled with his briefcase, of course, but he should have left something behind, apart from a few clothes, and there was nothing in the pockets of the jackets, because Daisy went through them all.

Either he was scrupulous about keeping all personal papers with him, or he had some other domicile, and whichever it was was suspicious. This place was too depersonalised. Looking around, Daisy said crisply, 'I wonder if he wipes his fingerprints off every morning. We're not learning anything from here.'

They came out of the barn and locked the door, then went into the cottage and sat down, surveying each other gloomily.

'What next?' asked Alison.

Daisy said, 'I know his car number, we might be able to track that down, and I thought I'd go back to the hotel where we saw that man yesterday. It was Sunday lunchtime and if he's local he probably comes in regularly, and if I describe him and where he sat I might be able to get his name.'

It was a chance. 'Failing everything,' she went on, briskly, 'I'll put a private detective on him.'

Alison gulped. 'We will?'

'I will,' said Daisy. Alison was not happy about this suggestion. Uncle Bob would be furious and so would Keith. It could start all sorts of gossip and scandal, and she said, 'I don't think we ought to get outsiders involved. Suppose he is Richard Lingard, and suppose he doesn't have any skeletons in the cupboard?'

'I think he does,' said Daisy, 'although he may well be Andrew's grandson. But private detectives have to be discreet, he'd never know he was being investigated.' She felt some trepidation herself as she said that; she couldn't imagine anyone shadowing Richard unmarked by those piercing dark Lingard eyes. It would be a last resort, calling in the professionals.

'Where would you find a private detective?' Alison wondered fearfully.

'Probably in the yellow pages,' said Daisy.

There were six listed under 'Detective Agencies', one in the town where Daisy worked, and she passed the door with a brass plate outside 'Registered Bailiff. Private Inquiries—Confidential', during her lunch hour. She had never noticed it before, and she hoped she wouldn't have to open the door and walk down the passage, and explain to someone waiting there that she wanted a man, who was not husband nor business colleague, investigated.

Today she was making for the *Redford Post*. Richard was a photographer, and newspapers knew about photographers. This was a small paper, but it was part of a bigger group, and they might have heard of him.

Daisy would have found what she was seeking eventually. With determination there were any number of ways she could have tracked it down, but it came so terribly easily.

She went up to the Features room where Maggie was at her desk, with a mug of tea and a cheese roll at her elbow. 'Hello,' Maggie greeted her. 'Have you got something for us?'

Daisy hadn't done any writing lately. 'This is a social call,' she said. 'Is Jack Brady around? I want to ask him if he's heard of a photographer called Richard Lingard. An American.'

'A relation?'

'Sort of.'

Maggie phoned the photographic department and asked, and shook her head. 'Sorry,' she said. 'They don't seem to have done.'

'He's small-time.' As she said that it seemed to Daisy a ludicrous description.

Maggie was smiling at her. 'I've been wanting to see you. Look at this.' She opened the bottom drawer of her desk and flipped through photographs. 'He was at a reception I went to in London,' she said. 'Richard Judd.'

'Who's he?' Daisy had heard the name, but the rest eluded her in a slight memory block.

'The newspaper tycoon,' said Maggie. 'You don't see many pictures of him, he's anti-personality cult, but what does he remind you of?'

'A dark Lingard,' said Daisy. He looked good in evening dress, distinguished and elegant. He looked in charge, the two men photographed with him were overshadowed. He was good at overshadowing.

'That's what I thought, 'said Maggie, laughing. 'In fact I asked him if he'd got any ancestors round here, but he hasn't. Isn't it a pity?'

'A tycoon in the family would have been useful,' said Daisy. 'Please may I have this?'

She came out of the office with the photograph. It was

134

Richard, there was no doubt at all, and she didn't need the reference library at work to fill in the details about him. She remembered them now.

Richard L. Judd. L for Lingard? Newspaper tycoon, top man of an international combine, with a reputation for brilliance and ruthlessness, and keeping out of the limelight.

So why hadn't he told them who he was? To preserve his privacy by an incognito? Because he was filthy rich and he didn't want relations sponging on him? As if they would, as if he couldn't see how fiercely independent Uncle Bob was, and Keith too. Or because he was getting more laughs around Oak House Farm than he had had in years? That was what he had told her, pretending to be a near-layabout and watching their reactions.

Daisy felt as though she was reeling, walking around town, using her lunch hour trying to calm herself down before she was due back in the library. He had made fools of them all, and that was why she was seething.

She never considered that the shock she had just experienced might have been loss. She had always believed that Richard Lingard had come to stay, but Richard L. Judd was out of her orbit.

CHAPTER SEVEN

ALISON looked at the photograph, then goggled as recognition hit her. 'It's *Richard*! Where did you get it?'

Daisy had phoned Oak House during the afternoon, and asked Alison to meet her at the cottage. 'I've something to show you,' she'd said, and hung up because she couldn't discuss it then. But Alison had been waiting when she got back from work, asking eagerly as Daisy stepped out of the car,

'You've found out something, haven't you? What have you found?'

'I'll show you,' Daisy had said, going into the cottage kitchen, where she took the photograph out of the magazine she was carrying it in and put it on the table.

'It's *Richard*!' shrilled Alison. 'Where did you get it?'

'From the *Redford Post*.'

'He looks very handsome,' said Alison grudgingly. 'When was it taken? I suppose it's too much to hope he's a crook?'

'Would you settle for a millionaire?' said Daisy.

'You don't mean that?'

Daisy picked up the photograph, studying the face. The thick dark straight hair fell in the way she knew, and she would never touch it again. The tenderness and the passion had been expertise, no more. This man had a world of women to choose from and there was an ache inside her like a cold and heavy stone. She said, 'Meet Richard L. Judd, who owns a string of newspapers, here and in America.' She added ironically, 'Photography must be one of his hobbies.'

Alison groped for a chair and sat down limply. 'Thank heaven!' she breathed. 'Are you sure?'

'That's him, isn't it? Well, that's who he is.'

Alison's face softened as the anxiety of the past weeks left her. She wondered, almost dreamily, 'Why didn't he tell us who he really was?'

'I've never been a tycoon, so I wouldn't know,' said Daisy, 'but he sets store on privacy, so that's probably why he's passing himself off as plain Richard Lingard here. What I can't understand is what you heard Uncle Bob saying to him, about the will. Why would Richard Judd bother about inheriting half a small farm he could buy a hundred times over?'

'Yes,' said Alison. 'Well ...' She bent over Woo and began to rub his tummy so that he squirmed happily. 'About that,' she said, spacing her words with a little silence between each, and keeping her head down so that she didn't meet Daisy's eyes, 'I didn't exactly hear what I told you. Not exactly those words.'

'*What?*' Daisy gasped.

'Uncle Bob did tell Richard he was seeing Laurenson, and Mr Laurenson is his lawyer, and I thought it must be about his will.' Alison stole a quick glance at Daisy, whose indignation was about to burst on her, and began to talk faster. 'Well, wouldn't you have thought it was? You warned me that Richard could be trying to oust Keith. You put the idea into my head, and when I heard Uncle Bob talking about seeing a lawyer I was sure it was about Andrew's share, and you were the only one who could help me and I had to make you believe he was changing his will. I believed it.' She drew breath, and Daisy put a hand in front of her eyes, suddenly drained, wanting to shut out everything.

'He could have been,' wailed Alison. Daisy nodded. 'But if Richard's that rich,' said Alison meekly, 'he isn't likely to

137

sell us up, is he? Don't you think he'd be more likely to invest in the farm?'

'I wouldn't know,' said Daisy again.

'You're angry. I'm sorry.' Alison felt reprieved by the news that Oak House Farm was no prize to Richard, he wouldn't be scheming to get a share of it; but now she wished that she had confined herself to repeating what Uncle Bob had actually said: 'I'm seeing Laurenson at eleven,' instead of adding 'and having everything divided equally between you and Keith.'

Daisy would probably have put the same interpretation on Uncle Bob's visit to his lawyer that Alison had, but Alison had stampeded her into yesterday's fiasco.

'I'm sorry,' Alison repeated plaintively, then offered, 'Shall I tell Richard I asked you to lead him on, that it was my idea?' She quailed as she imagined herself doing that, and when Daisy demanded,

'What good would that do?' she breathed more freely, although she had to suggest,

'Perhaps he wouldn't blame you then.'

'It wouldn't make one scrap of difference,' said Daisy. 'I thought he was taking over as much as you did, and it might have been your idea, but I was the girl——' the lump in her throat was hard to swallow. 'The girl who gave the performance,' she said.

Alison had stopped tickling Woo, and was looking again at the photograph of Richard. 'It's beastly bad luck, because I think he really liked you.'

Yesterday Daisy had believed that too, but he hadn't liked her or trusted her enough to tell her his name, and he had been cynical enough to come out of their lovemaking ice-calm. Any feeling he had for her was superficial. She said bitterly, 'He fancied me—he could have been serious about that proposition.'

'You mean asking you to marry him?' Alison's eyes

brightened with a sudden excitement that Daisy was almost sorry to dampen.

'Not quite,' she said. 'There was nothing serious about the proposal. This was a proposition, that if he needed a mistress he'd let me know.'

'Oh!' Alison didn't know what to make of that. It was a glimpse into another way of life. Love and marriage were her world, and she wanted them for Daisy. 'Would you——?' she whispered.

'Most unlikely,' said Daisy briskly, and remembered that first morning, standing with Richard under the painting of Hugo, discussing if they would ever make friends. 'Most unlikely,' he had said. Yesterday they had seemed like friends, but she would never be at ease with him again. She said, 'I'm old-fashioned, you see. Uncle Bob's not the only one out of *East Lynne*.'

She did not say that it would be emotional suicide to get involved with a man who could break her heart, and watch it shatter with detachment and even amusement.

'Do we tell him we've seen this?' Alison indicated the photograph, and Daisy picked it up and put it in a drawer of the dresser. The Chinese lion sat there, and Alison asked, 'Wherever did that come from?'

'Richard bought it for me yesterday, and no, we don't say we know who he is.' Daisy wondered if Uncle Bob had been told and thought not. 'Let's see how long he takes to tell us. Besides, he's enjoying himself here.' She banged the dresser drawer so that the Chinese lion jerked a little and she had to move quickly to steady it. 'He told me he was getting more laughs than he's had in years.'

'Is that good?'

'Hilarious,' said Daisy. 'I always enjoy being made a fool of.'

'We tried to make a fool of him,' Alison ventured, and Daisy pulled a face.

'And oh, my golly, weren't we out of our depth? Well,

now you know that you're the poor relations, not him, there's no panic.'

'I must tell Keith,' said Alison eagerly, and of course she must. She had told Keith what she had overheard Uncle Bob say about seeing Mr Laurenson, without the invented rider. But Keith had agreed that it was pretty sure Uncle Bob was changing his will, and it would come as a tremendous relief to him to hear that Richard was no fortune-hunter. He would say he had known all along. Not of course that Richard was Richard Judd, but that he had had no designs on the farm.

Alison jumped up. She wanted to run all the way home with this super secret, which should be making everything happy again, although Daisy wasn't smiling. 'He's bound to tell us before long, isn't he?' she said, and Daisy shrugged.

'Not if he doesn't want us to know.'

Uncle Bob didn't know. Keith and Alison went out after the evening meal, to a bistro on the river where there was dancing. They asked Daisy to go with them, but she didn't feel like dancing, and it was nice to see them dash off together, almost carefree again.

Nanny took a patchwork quilt she was repairing, to sit in front of the television in the small sitting room. Daisy might have watched television too, but Uncle Bob stayed in the kitchen reading a farming magazine, so she brought out a writing pad and began to answer a letter.

After a few minutes she said, 'Uncle Bob, about Richard.'

'Aye?'

'How much do you know about him?'

He smiled at her, pleased with this sign that Richard was on her mind, although he had been annoyed when Alison put the same question.

'All I need to know,' he said, 'to say you could do a lot worse than Richard. He'd look after you and you might even be able to persuade him to settle down here.' He refilled his pipe and drew on it, nodding over a dream. 'When I'm gone he and Keith might work the farm together, and he could always go on taking the photographs.'

That didn't sound as though he knew that Richard was an international press tycoon, and he wasn't hiding anything or it would have shown on his broad and honest face. He had taken Richard on trust for what he said he was, Andrew Lingard's grandson, a roaming freelance photographer.

Daisy said, 'You haven't really ever asked for proof that he's a Lingard, have you? He could be an impostor.'

Robert chuckled. 'If he is he's not getting much out of it. I'd have put him in my will for his grandfather's sake, but he wouldn't hear of it. Put his foot right down. This place belongs to Keith, he said, all of it, but if you said the word Daisy-girl we might persuade him to stay here.'

Daisy said, 'He's quite famous, you know. I don't think he'd ever give up his work.'

'Famous, is he?' Robert Lingard was pleased but not surprised. He teased her jovially, 'Well, you're going to be a famous writer one day, aren't you? He can take the pictures for you.'

'When I'm famous I'll ask him,' she said lightly. She wondered what would happen to the photographs Richard took yesterday, if she would ever see them, if they would betray her. Because almost all that day long she had been falling in love with him.

That week she researched on Richard L. Judd. She told nobody why. Only Alison and Keith knew the identity of Richard Lingard, and, because they knew, the atmosphere at Oak House had lightened, the shadows had gone.

Alison's was a resilient nature, and Daisy had said that Richard had been amused by their attempts to blacklist him with Uncle Bob. He could afford to laugh, the joke was on them, and when he returned at the weekend he would no longer be a threat, he would be accepted on his own terms. If he wanted to be plain Richard Lingard he was Richard

Lingard. That was how Alison saw the situation.

In fact he was Richard L. Judd—it was always the initial, never the full middle name—and at the age of eighteen he had started his career on a small Wisconsin newspaper owned by his mother's father, Edgar Judd. Almost self-made, with the luck of the born winner, formidable talent and energy, he had acquired a press empire over the following decade.

Daisy read all she could about him, from reference books and back numbers of magazines and newspapers. She was still telling herself her interest was curiosity; and that her pride was irked because his deception had made fools of them. She fooled herself most of the time.

It didn't help when Uncle Bob wanted to know if she'd heard from Richard. 'Of course not,' she said. Undeterred, Uncle Bob assured her,

'Well, you'll be seeing him again at the weekend.'

That was what Richard had written in the note he'd left for her, but that was no love letter. He would return at the weekend because he had a retreat here from the jet-set rat-race, and probably because he was fond of Uncle Bob, and Keith and Nanny. But not to see Daisy. Except perhaps for laughs, because Daisy amused him.

She worked extra energetically, and went out most evenings, but she had no fun at all. Her dates never guessed it, she seemed her usual bubbling self, but she felt wretchedly low all the time, and she was sleeping badly.

On Friday the roses came, delivered to Oak House during the afternoon. When Daisy walked into the kitchen after work they were in a plastic bucket on the draining board, two dozen long-stemmed red roses.

'They're gorgeous,' said Daisy, sniffing a bud. 'Why don't you put them in a vase? Did Keith bring them for you?' And Alison, who had been waiting for this ever since the roses arrived, said nonchalantly,

'You put them in a vase—they're yours.'

142

Daisy had had flowers sent to her before, but it wasn't her birthday, and she wasn't expecting flowers. 'Who from?' she asked, looking for the card, which read, 'For Daisy, from Richard.'

'Isn't that nice of him?' Alison was thrilled. At the least it was a peace-offering. 'When I read the card,' she gloated, 'I wondered if you knew another Richard, but you don't, do you? It is our Richard, isn't it?'

Our Richard? *The* Richard L. Judd, who was very much his own man and certainly belonged to no one here. Daisy said, 'It must be him. I wonder why.'

'Why do men usually send girls red roses?' Alison had opened the big brown cupboard that contained most of the household china not in every day use, and produced a couple of vases from the bottom shelf, one cut glass, one Willow Pattern Victorian.

'Either of these do?' She held them up for inspection and Daisy took the Willow Pattern, filled it, and lifted the roses dripping from their bucket.

'Red roses for true love,' she said. 'I wonder how many true loves Richard Judd could call on any hour of the day or night.' She gave a little 'ouch!' of pain as a thorn scratched her, and looked at her thumb and the drop of blood, the colour of roses.

'Beware of gifts with thorns,' she said shakily.

But everyone else was delighted with the roses. Uncle Bob beamed over them all through dinner. '*Very* nice,' said Keith, and Nanny even suggested that Daisy should pick out the prettiest rose of all and press it, to add to the other faded and fragile flowers that women from a bygone age had put between the leaves of books still on the shelves of Oak House.

No one knew exactly when Richard would be returning, but he arrived on Saturday evening. Daisy had been out, at a girl friend's, and when she came back his car was outside the barn. She panicked and drove on to the house; she couldn't face him alone. If she went into the cottage he might be in the barn and come round. If he was in the house there would be others around.

He was in the house. In the drawing room, with the family and the dogs and old Josh; and two more callers, a middle-aged couple who kept the village store and had met Richard before as Richard Lingard. When Daisy appeared in the doorway they were grouped round Richard.

She'd seen it before, he had always been the dominant personality, and what she knew about him now explained that. Of course he towered over anyone he was likely to meet here.

She stood in the doorway, and his eyes swept over her, head to foot. She was wearing a new dress, with a white sleeveless tube top and a sunray-pleated skirt. She looked as good as she could, on the money she could afford. He was in thin grey sweater and slacks, part of his 'slumming' gear. In the few photographs she had seen of him this week he had been impeccably dressed: silk shirts, superbly cut suits.

'Hello,' he said.

'Hello to you.' She came in, smiling warily. 'Thank you for the roses. Did you have a good week?'

Alison said quickly, 'He's been taking some aerial photographs.' From his own plane, no doubt, thought Daisy sourly. Obviously his account of his week was deliberately misleading again, and although Alison and Keith were pretending to believe every word Daisy had an upsurge of resentment.

'Tell me about it,' she said.

'I'll show you the pictures.'

'That would be fascinating.' Her edginess showed. Uncle Bob and Nanny were putting it down to bashfulness, Alison and Keith were hoping that Daisy was not going to blurt out what she had discovered since she last saw Richard. They had talked about it a great deal and decided to leave

144

things as they were. If Richard learned that Alison and Daisy had been inquiring about him he might walk out, and now they knew he wasn't plotting to take the farm away from them they were glad he was part of the family. As Keith had said—until the problem of the will came up—he was a capital chap and damn good company. They were proud of him now too, and certain he would take them into his confidence in his own time.

But Daisy knew him better than they did. She was the one he had told he was getting more laughs here, and she sat and fumed through the next hour. How long did he think he could get away with it? Eventually someone would have tracked him down here, or his picture would have turned up in a paper. Suppose she had brought Maggie along with her tonight? That would have done it. Or produced the photograph Maggie had given her. She had the proof that he was more devious than she could ever be, hiding his real name and his true identity, as though his relatives could be trusted with neither.

At their last meeting he had done all he could to humiliate her, and he was still doing it. The note and the roses were all part of the joke, that he was crazy about her. Suppose she said now, 'I've been thinking about that proposal of marriage you made me in front of Uncle Bob and I've decided to accept, because it isn't every day a girl gets a chance to become Mrs Richard Judd.'

As soon as the visitors left she might give herself the treat of disconcerting him. He disconcerted her, all the time. Seeing his car outside the barn, walking into this room, looking at him, speaking to him, made her feel churned up and worn out. And angry. She hung on to anger because it was warming and without it she would have been cold.

'All I know for sure about you is that you're a liar,' she had told him. She said that again now, silently—you're a liar. And he smiled that crooked smile at her and it pierced her, like the thorn on the rose but reaching her heart.

If she said, 'I'll marry you, Richard Lingard,' then he would have to say, 'I didn't mean a word of it.' He would have to say she was not up to his standards. He would know she knew, and he would have to tell them who he was.

She was suddenly determined he should tell them. But if she produced the photograph or simply called him by his full name he would handle that coolly, he must have been expecting something like that any time. She wanted him taken aback, thrown off keel if only for a minute or two, and she stayed where she was because Alison was angling to get her out of the room.

When Richard's opinion was asked, on a private Member's bill on a country matter at present before Parliament, Richard said, 'I'm no expert,' and Daisy chimed in sweetly,

'Maybe not, but I'm sure you know whole teams of experts.'

'Drink, Daisy?' Keith suggested. The others were sitting holding their glasses, except Nanny who had a yellow mug of hot milk.

'No, thanks,' said Daisy.

'Coffee, then?' offered Alison. 'Tea?' Either would have enabled her to get Daisy into the kitchen to help make it, but Daisy shook her head.

'I've just had supper and an awful lot of tea at Janet's.'

Richard turned with a raised eyebrow. 'A date with a girl on Saturday night?'

'Why not?' said Daisy, still sweet as sugar. 'I do have girl friends as well. We're not all lone wolves.' Alison was sure she was going to ask him why he never brought any friends here and said shrilly,

'Daisy, could you——?' She beckoned, signalling come here, come outside, shut up.

'What?' said Daisy, sitting tight.

'I want you a minute.'

'Won't it wait?'

Alison drew in a deep breath, wondering how she could say, 'No, it won't,' without communicating her urgency, when Mrs Bicknell glanced down at her watch and said,

'It's getting late. I hadn't noticed how the time was going. We'd best be getting along home.'

Her husband finished his drink and stood up with her. So did old Josh, and after the usual goodnights Alison and Keith saw the three visitors to the front door. As they walked away Alison murmured, 'Daisy's going to tell Richard we know who he is any minute.'

Keith put a consoling arm around her and asked, 'Does it matter?'

'How she breaks the news might matter,' said Alison dolefully.

Keith would much rather have let things take their own course. Daisy had been indignant at the subterfuge practised on them, but Keith couldn't see that Richard had done any harm by playing down his power and position. Keith liked him better for it.

He said regretfully, 'Daisy's always been set against Richard, hasn't she? Although he's been very decent to her, sending her roses.'

The red roses were on a table in the hall, and as they closed the front door Daisy came into the hall and took a flower. She had turned back into the drawing room before Alison could have reached her. It was no use calling, in Daisy's present mulish frame of mind, so Alison hurried after her.

Daisy went straight to Richard, still sitting in a black oak carved armchair, and said, 'I'd like to have given you one of these. Aren't they beautiful? It was so thoughtful of you to send them. But you don't have a buttonhole, do you? Don't you ever wear a decent suit?'

'Only for business.' He stood up and took the rose from her, laying it on the tray on which Nanny had collected the empty glasses. Nanny had just been leaving the room

147

with them, but now she stood still, the tray in her hands, waiting to hear what was coming next.

Keith followed Alison into the room and Daisy said gaily, 'Isn't it cosy now all the outsiders have gone, and it's just the family? It's lovely to have you home again.'

She reached up to kiss Richard's cheek, very lightly, then stepped back quickly, laughing at Nanny and Keith. 'Did that surprise you? You're not surprised are you, Uncle Bob? You know that Richard asked me to marry him. Well, I'm thinking about it very seriously.'

That broke like a small bombshell. Everybody was jolted so that they could only gasp and croak. Including Alison, who had expected almost anything but this. Not including Uncle Bob, of course, he was looking delighted; and Richard didn't look as poleaxed as Daisy had hoped.

It was impossible to tell what Richard was thinking, but his smile didn't falter, and when Uncle Bob smiled, 'There's a good girl!' Richard said,

'A very good girl,' and kissed her, as lightly as she had kissed him.

She went on, in the same bright voice, 'I've been thinking about you all week. You asked me in your note to think about you. Have you thought about me?'

'Constantly,' he said.

She fluttered lashes at him. 'And you must have had such a lot of other things to think about, because you're such a busy man, aren't you?'

'Oh yes.' He looked at all of them. 'You will excuse us, won't you?' he said. 'We have things to discuss.'

He took Daisy's arm, and she shrugged and went with him. She was going home anyway, and if he still wanted to keep his identity secret he'd have to produce some good reasons to ensure her silence. That was probably what he wanted to discuss.

Richard loosed Daisy as soon as they were out of the front door, and they walked silently under a moon covered by scudding clouds, so that one moment seemed light as dawn and another quite dark. Then she said, 'It's your move next,' and he pulled her into his arms, kissing her mouth, engulfing her in darkness.

Almost before she realised what was happening, although she had instinctively stiffened, pushing flat palms against his chest, he released her. The moon shone down again and he was laughing. 'I'm sure you don't believe in sex before marriage,' he said, 'but not even a kiss?'

'Not the way you kiss.' His kisses could take over her mind, it had happened before. She was breathing fast now, and she turned to walk on down the track, spotting Woo under her feet just in time to avoid tripping full length over him. Beside her Richard asked with a sidelong grin, 'What kind of wife will you make some frustrated man, Daisy Penrose?'

He meant she would be unresponsive, and he was wrong. In him she had discovered an intensity of sexual attraction she hadn't known existed. She had been called frigid by men who left her cold. Now here was one who could unlock her senses, and it was her best safeguard that he should never know that. She said coolly, 'Not your style of wife at all,' and after a tiny pause to emphasise it, 'Richard Lingard.'

'Well, finish the name,' he said. 'Richard Lingard Judd, your cover is blown.'

'The L does stand for Lingard, then?'

'Yes.'

'Are you surprised we've found out?'

'No. It was bound to happen sooner or later.'

'You wouldn't have told us?'

'Possibly.' They walked side by side, as though they were taking a late night stroll, and their conversation sounded casual. 'How did you find out?' Richard asked her. 'Was it your friend Miss Cookson from the *Post*?'

'Yes.'

149

He laughed wryly. 'I told her I had no relations here, but I thought she might check.'

'She believed you, but she showed me a photograph because you looked like a dark Lingard.'

He swore, but as though he was amused rather than angry. 'So I'm in that follow-up story after all.'

'Maggie still doesn't know,' said Daisy. 'I didn't tell her. I just agreed with her about your face.'

'Well, thank you for that,' he said. 'Who did you tell? Alison and Keith—and I appreciated the way they pretended they didn't know tonight. But if Robert and Nanny are in the know the old-time stage missed a couple of talented troupers.'

They were nearing the cottage and the barn, and when Daisy stepped into her home she would shut the door on him, so the talking must be finished before then. 'Uncle Bob and Nanny still don't know,' she said stiffly. 'You made fools of us.'

'You made a fool of yourself,' he retorted. 'I'm Andrew Lingard's illegitimate grandson, exactly as I told you. And tell me who's any worse off because I dropped the Judd from my name?'

She thought she might be. If she had known from the beginning that he was Richard L. Judd she would not have let herself become involved. She had been content with her life, now she had longings that would never be satisfied—a loss, a loneliness. She thought that she was a great deal worse off, but she couldn't tell him that. She said accusingly, 'You told me you were going to be master here.'

'I don't take kindly to being conned. I'd have pulled the place down around your ears that night if I could have done. I didn't mean it, I've got enough going. But I wouldn't mind an interest in the farm.' He walked a little ahead of her, leaving the track, going between the trees. 'As a sleeping partner, if you'll pardon the expression.'

That would be ideal, for the farm and the house. She said

quietly, to his back, 'Alison overheard Uncle Bob telling you he was seeing his lawyer, and we thought it was about changing his will.'

'You do jump to conclusions, dragging poor Alison along with you.'

'Alison has a mind of her own,' Daisy protested.

'Of course she has. But she's not a match for you. You're twice as tough as she is.' Nobody had ever thought that before. It was no compliment, but it could be true. Richard went towards the barn and Daisy hurried past him to the door of the cottage. 'Robert was selling me the barn,' said Richard. 'That's why he saw the lawyer.'

'Oh!' As she fumbled in her purse for her key she muttered, 'I'm—sorry. We thought if Uncle Bob thought you were—promiscuous it might—put him off you.'

'Promiscuous?' It was quiet enough for his voice to reach her as though they were still standing close enough to touch, and there was enough light to see him clearly at the door of the barn.

'Aren't you?' she said.

'No.' He added nothing, but he could have said, 'Selective, with the best to choose from.' From what Daisy had read in her research of Richard L. Judd she couldn't hold a candle to the women he went around with. She said,

'Anyhow, it was that article I wrote that brought you here and I felt I'd sort of conjured you up, and you were putting Keith into second place.'

'Not intentionally.'

He couldn't help overshadowing Keith. She only hoped he wasn't going to put every other man she met into second place. He had so far.

'And you didn't conjure me up,' he said. 'I've been around a few years longer than you.' As she opened the door of the cottage he said, 'I'll tell Robert and Nanny tomorrow that I've got another name.'

'It won't make any difference to them.' Daisy was sure of

that. 'It won't make any difference to anyone here. Alison and Keith are glad you're not taking the farm away from them, but of course Keith didn't think you were, and you're right about Alison—she wouldn't have done if I hadn't scared her about the dark Lingards.'

'And you?' he queried.

'I'm glad you're not after the farm—I thought you were. Apart from that, what difference could it make to me what you do for a living?'

'None,' he said. 'Goodnight.'

'Goodnight.' But of course it made an immense difference, an immense gulf, and he must know it. He had bought the barn, so he meant to stay here some of the time, but Richard L. Judd had apartments in London and Montreal and New York, and an ocean-going boat. So this would only be one more port of call. That talk of putting down roots had been part of the role he was playing.

Daisy got ready for bed, scowling at herself every time she passed a mirror. Richard had enjoyed kissing her again just now, and he would make love to her if she let him. There was another gulf between them. For him the love-making would be sensuous, entirely physical. It would leave no mark on his mind, while it might leave her needing him for the rest of her life.

That day, last Sunday, they had spent together, there had been signs that this could develop as no other relationship for her. Last Sunday had been like the beginning of a journey into an enchanted land. She had wanted to know him, everything about him, every way, and now she knew his name and the voyage of discovery was over.

She was pretty enough for Richard L. Judd to fancy her, but she didn't want to be fancied. She wanted to be loved, to the exclusion of all other women, and she didn't have that kind of magic. She cried in her sleep that night. She couldn't remember her dreams, but her cheeks were wet when she woke and her eyelids were pink and puffy.

Her appearance horrified her. She couldn't let anyone see her looking like this, so she put cold compresses on her eyes to reduce the puffiness, and made up with more than usual care and skill before she dared even open the door to let the dogs out. Richard might be walking around, or he might open his door. He mustn't see red eyes for pity's sake, and if she had to cry why hadn't she wept her tears while he was away?

She knew why. Seeing him had stripped away her delusions, and made her admit to herself that she wanted him, and she could only have him on terms that would destroy her. So she made up very carefully, and combed her hair into a feathery fringe that hid her eyes a little.

She ate half a grapefruit and two rounds of toast, although often as not she skipped breakfast altogether, and on Sundays she usually walked up to the house and took pot luck there. She wasn't sure whether she was putting off facing them all, or acting perversely because you were supposed to starve with a hopeless love affair.

The toast tasted like cardboard and each gulp was an effort, but she got it down, and she was sitting staring at the crumbs on her plate when the dogs began to bark and there was the hoot of a car's horn outside.

It was Uncle Bob's car, he and Nanny sat in front, she in one of her best hats. Nanny's window was wound down, and she called, 'Are you coming to church?' as Daisy opened the cottage door.

Daisy shook her head and Nanny tutted. 'Then you might as well go and give Alison a hand with the vegetables,' she said, and wound her window up again.

There was no sign of Richard, and Daisy washed up her breakfast things and walked up the track to the house. The sun shone and the birds sang and the house wasn't threatened any more, so it should have been a beautiful morning.

Alison was in the kitchen, in her white bibbed apron, stirring currants into a pudding mixture in a big mixing

153

bowl. She greeted Daisy with, 'What *are* you playing at?'

'Who's around?' asked Daisy. 'I've seen Uncle Bob and Nanny.'

'Keith's somewhere about. Richard hasn't been here this morning.' Alison went on stirring automatically with her wooden spoon, demanding, 'Why did you say that last night? What happened? I didn't like to come down to the cottage in case you'd made him angry again—I didn't think it would help if I turned up.' She grimaced. 'Not after last time.'

'He isn't mad,' said Daisy. She tipped a few currants from the packet and fed them to herself one by one. 'And I said he'd asked me to marry him because I wanted to make him admit that Richard L. Judd is in the market for a mistress maybe but not for a wife. Well, not for a wife the likes of me.'

'What did he say?' Alison still stirred, but Daisy had all her attention.

'He'd realised you and Keith know who he is,' said Daisy, 'and he thinks it was nice of you to pretend you didn't. He's telling Uncle Bob and Nanny this morning. Everything's above board now. No more secrets.' She offered a currant to Woo and Cooch, who both surveyed them with suspicion. Woo went on snuffling his around the kitchen floor, Cooch left his and settled down on a rug. 'What shall I do?' asked Daisy. 'The greens or the potatoes?'

'Oh—either.' Daisy sounded cheerful and Alison was beginning to believe that the bad patch was really over. She couldn't be sure until she had seen Richard, but it would be wonderful if nobody had to pretend any more. Richard had spotted that she and Keith were putting on an act last night, which proved they weren't too good at pretending.

Daisy was humming a tune as she scraped the potatoes, as though she hadn't a care in the world. It was just like it used to be, Alison thought.

Richard crossed the courtyard a few minutes later and

154

Alison, at the window, turned to warn Daisy, 'Here's Richard.'

'Three more potatoes,' said Daisy, 'if he's staying to lunch,' and she scraped on quite steadily, even when the kitchen door opened and her heart was anything but steady.

Richard came into the room, and went across to Alison. When he smiled she smiled too, looking young and pretty and slightly apprehensive. 'I should be apologising,' he said.

'Whatever for?' she asked.

'I wasn't altogether honest with you.' His smile, appealing, disarming, included Daisy. 'But I very much appreciated somewhere I could get right away, with no business problems following me. And I *am* Richard Lingard, and you are all the family I have, so I hope you don't feel that I practised an unforgivable deception.'

'No,' said Alison. '*No ...*'

Richard hugged her. 'You're a great girl,' he smiled. He might have hugged Daisy, but she was farther away, and moved farther still, drying her hands busily.

'We won't tell a soul if you don't want us to,' Alison promised, and he grinned wryly.

'It couldn't have gone on much longer, could it? So long as it makes no difference to you folk here.'

'Why ever should it?' asked Alison.

'Are you eating lunch with us?' asked Daisy.

'Please,' said Richard.

Why does he talk such nonsense, thought Daisy, when he knows it must change everything?

Uncle Bob and Nanny took the news calmly over lunch. So Richard was Richard Lingard Judd, of whom neither of them had heard anyway. When he told them his mother's father had owned the small newspaper which had 'led to bigger things', Nanny quoted sagely, 'Big oaks from little acorns grow,' as though it was a natural and simple procedure.

But Keith was looking at Richard with admiring awe. 'The pressure must be killing,' said Keith.

'It can be,' Richard agreed. 'The boat was my main escape hatch until I came here.'

Now he escaped to Oak House Farm, a quiet village backwater, instead of riding the high seas. He told them about the boat, and Daisy wondered if he remembered that the first dark Lingard was said to have been a pirate.

A motor-sailer, berthing six comfortably, didn't sound like a pirate craft, but it did sound a wonderful thing to have and Keith, who would have enjoyed messing about in boats if he had been able to afford a boat, hung enthralled on Richard's description.

'Well, there it is,' said Richard. 'I'm hoping to get away in it myself before too long. A week or two around some islands in the sun. Why don't you come?'

He meant Keith and Alison and Daisy, and Keith and Alison were in the seventh heaven at the idea. So was Daisy. At least she supposed she was. It sounded like a wonderful holiday.

'Wonderful!' breathed Alison, clasping her hands in delight, and laughing at Richard. 'Not that we know much about boats, although we did hire a longboat one summer for a week, and had a super time, although it never stopped raining. Remember?'

Daisy and Keith remembered. Three years ago with three others. 'Daisy swims like a fish,' said Alison.

'A swimming pool fish,' said Daisy. 'Not an ocean-going fish.' A girl for the shallows, not the deep. She could imagine Richard's friends who used the boat, clever, successful, beautiful people. Keith and Alison would be accepted, because they were young and attractive themselves, and Richard's family.

Am I his family? Daisy wondered. As Keith is my brother will I ever feel that way about Richard? It wasn't likely, but she had better start working on it.

'Fancy you having a boat like that!' said Nanny.

'And a plane,' said Daisy laconically. 'And three homes, isn't it? Four with the barn.'

Uncle Bob's grizzled eyebrows rose, at the extent of Richard's success. '*Four* homes?'

'London. Philadelphia. Montreal,' Daisy babbled. She wished she could be quiet, but her nerves were jangling and she couldn't stop chattering.

'Who looks after them?' asked Nanny. 'Who lives in them if you haven't got a wife or a family?' She added sharply, suddenly unsure if they had been misled on that matter too, 'You haven't, have you?'

'No,' said Richard. 'And they're serviced apartments, not houses. I use them when I need them.'

'You never married?' With all this Richard would have the women after him, Robert reckoned, but Richard smiled and shook his head.

'No, but neither did you. You're an old bachelor and you look happy enough to me.'

Robert had been eligible in his day, but never as eligible as Richard. There had been the girl over whom he had quarrelled with Andrew, but he had never been alone. Oak House had always contained those who loved and needed him. He included Daisy and Alison as naturally as though they were born Lingards when he said, 'I've always had my family around me.' He chuckled, 'And I've never found a woman who'd put up with me like my family do.'

'I have my family too now,' said Richard, 'and it would have to be a very special woman who'd put up with me.'

Daisy saw Uncle Bob considering this, and she knew what he was thinking—that she was special here, but not in the world Richard L. Judd inhabited.

True enough, she thought. Uncle Bob can't see me winging between Montreal and London, keeping Richard's mind off gorgeous determined females. No man was too good for Daisy in Uncle Bob's mind, but Richard was too

157

rich. He had wanted the struggling photographer for her, not the self-made tycoon. The right catch for Daisy was along the speckled trout lines, and Richard L. Judd was a man-eating shark.

Daisy ate her lunch. They all ate with good appetites, and Richard answered questions, candidly this time, telling them all they wanted to know about him. Daisy had run out of chatter. She concentrated on getting the food down, and looking interested, but no more. Not stricken, not sick at heart because of the gulf that widened between them with everything he said, so that he moved farther and farther away from her.

He sat by her, at the kitchen table. She wondered vaguely whether Nanny would lay the meals he ate with them in the dining room, now they knew he was a millionaire, and knew she wouldn't. Money would make no difference to Nanny's attitude. But to Daisy it meant that he sat in the next chair and was unreachable.

She asked later if she could tell Maggie. 'When she does find out she's going to think I kept it from her, and she is a friend of mine.'

'Keep your imagination in check,' said Richard, 'and remember that all the proof you've got—apart from the way I look—is my middle name.'

He was in the study with Uncle Bob and Keith, and Daisy had gone in to say goodnight. Uncle Bob sat in his big swivel chair; but both Uncle Bob's chair and Keith's were turned towards Richard, sitting at the side of the desk with papers before him. He looked quizzically at Daisy. 'And Richard Lingard's letters to my mother,' he added, 'which are not for publication. Nor for comment.'

'Of course not,' she said. 'Well, goodnight, everybody.' She went round to kiss Uncle Bob's weatherbeaten cheek. She could have kissed Keith too. A peck on the cheek when she said goodnight would have meant no more than a smile, because Keith was her dear kind brother. And she hoped the day would come when she could touch Richard casually, without shaking inside.

'Having fun?' she asked, glancing at the papers on the desk as she walked round it, and they all smiled at her.

She walked down to the cottage alone, except for the dogs. Richard came back to the barn after she was in bed. Daisy had her window open and she heard his footsteps on the track in the silent night. Woo barked a little downstairs, Cooch stirred on the bedroom floor but, recognising the tread of a friend, gave a slow wag of a feathery tail and went back to sleep.

It was just after midnight by her small luminous clock. She sat up and thumped her pillow and asked it, 'Why can't you sleep in your London apartment while you're in England? What do you want with a barn anyway?' Then she buried her head in the pillow and tried to make her mind a blank, with such concentrated effort that sheer exhaustion put her to sleep at last.

Margaret Cookson was very surprised next day when Daisy came round to the *Post* offices during the lunch hour and told her what Richard L. Judd's initial stood for. It would have been quite a story, a dark Lingard tycoon turning up, if Richard's parents had married before his father died. As it was he had the middle name, and the looks, and was producing no proof and giving no interviews. His only quote for publication was that the Lingards of Oak House Farm might be his relations. He would be staying there occasionally and converting an old barn into a residence.

'Which barn?' Margaret asked Daisy.

'The barn on my cottage,' said Daisy.

Margaret whistled soundlessly. 'That'll put you and your cottage in a little millionaire's row!'

'I hope not,' said Daisy. 'I'd never live up to it.'

The barn hardly changed at all, from the outside. A local firm of builders descended on it and, with money no object and detailed instructions to follow, adapted and rebuilt the inside into a stylish studio home. In double quick time too. Richard was out of the country for three weeks, during which Daisy's home was filled with dust, and the frontage of her cottage was blocked with building materials and sightseers.

Family, farm workers, friends and neighbours all watched progress with great interest; and as the builders put in overtime until quite late at night Daisy kept Cooch at Oak House till her own bedtime. Continual voices and noises next door, after a lifetime of peaceful isolation, were infuriating him.

But on the date stipulated the barn was finished and the builders' bonus earned. It looked very good. Rugged stone-work contrasting with white walls, a big open fireplace, a pine staircase leading to a gallery and a couple of biggish bedrooms under the eaves. The floor was pine-blocked, a kitchen and a bathroom, small and superbly fitted, were behind a pine-panelled wall.

The furniture arrived in a large van, together with two husky men and a diagram where each item should be placed. Alison had a lovely time, stroking the furniture—soft leather and smooth wood—and changing a few pieces around because Richard had added a postcript to the list that Mrs Lingard was in charge and her instructions should be followed.

She tried to get Daisy involved; where did Daisy think this rug should be? and the desk to get the best light? Daisy stood in the middle of it all and saw Richard everywhere and opted out, repeating over and over again, 'I don't know, don't ask me.'

But she ached to participate. Sitting tight and taut, on one of the stone hummocks that were each side the fireplace, she wanted to put some mark on Richard's home. Then she thought of the other homes he had, and the other

160

women who must have influenced them, and she daren't compete.

'You're the homemaker,' she told Alison. 'It's all that decorating you've done.' She laughed, hugging her knees. 'If he wasn't in such a high-powered rush over everything you could have fixed this for him at half the price.'

'You're a nut,' said Alison happily. 'A pot of paint's my limit. This is splendid, isn't it?'

'Splendid,' agreed Daisy.

Alison left her there. It was a stupid thing to do. Stupid on Daisy's part to see the shadows fall in Richard's home. 'I'll sit here a bit longer,' she said when Alison had to get back to Oak House, because Keith and Uncle Bob would be in from the fields wanting their dinner. Nanny was cooking the meal. Alison had taken the afternoon off to see Richard's furniture in, but Keith would expect Alison there and Alison wanted to be where Keith wanted her.

'Make sure the door's shut,' was her parting request to Daisy. 'Dinner in about half an hour.'

Daisy sat for a while, by the empty fireplace. When logs were burning here the room would be glowing and warm. It was warm enough now, but there was a newness, an unused feeling about it, as though it waited to be turned from a showplace into a home. The smell of fresh paint and plaster lingered on the air, and she got to her feet at last and walked around.

She wondered what was new here, what Richard had used before. Not much, she thought. She wondered if he had selected, or if someone had been told to supply what would be needed, someone who knew his tastes.

The desk was lovely, walnut, and olive green tooled leather. And the oval dining table, with four chairs around it, where he had had one chair and an old scrubbed-top table. He could entertain around this, someone could cook in that well-equipped kitchen. Friends would be coming now, and if Daisy wasn't invited too she would know because Cooch would be on constant alert on the cottage side of the wall.

She looked at all the chairs around the table, almost seeing future guests in them. Then she went up the pine staircase and along the gallery, opening the doors, looking in on both bedrooms. Bed linen was in a wooden chest, Richard would probably see to that himself. Which was his room, which was his guest room? There was one bed in each room, big enough for two, and she had better go downstairs again. She mustn't let her imagination run riot up here.

The dogs were still at Oak House or they would have given her warning. As it was she was on the gallery, and goodness knows where her thoughts were, when down below the door opened and Richard walked in.

She froze, then drew back instinctively until she was against the wall. She had reasons for being here. She and Alison had supervised the moving in of the furniture. When her mouth was less dry she would call, 'Hello, welcome home,' but right now she couldn't make a sound.

He was alone. He closed the door behind him and stood looking around. The shadows were thick now, and as he crossed to a light switch Daisy took a deep breath. Now she *had* to say, 'Hello,' but before she could he said wearily,

'Come on down. I don't like being spied on.'

'I'm not spying on you!' Indignation moved her, verbally and physically, jerking her out of her frozen state, bringing her briskly down the stairs.

'Then stop lurking in the shadows,' he drawled. He turned on lights, and turned on her with a look that was unfriendly to say the least.

'And welcome home,' she snapped. 'And to heck with you too!'

They stood there, scowling at each other. The thick straight dark hair fell over his eyes, and he tossed it back and began to smile.

CHAPTER EIGHT

'SORRY,' said Richard. 'Put it down to jet-lag, it was a long trip.' There was a wryness about his grin, as though he had been told a bad joke. 'But this isn't bad at all,' he went on, looking around, shrugging off weariness.

'By my standards it's palatial,' said Daisy. 'Everybody thinks so.'

'How is everybody?'

'If you mean the family, they're very well.' He was wearing a fine hopsack suit, cream silk shirt, dark brown tie—the trappings of Richard L. Judd, not Richard Lingard.

'Dinner's ready up at the house,' she said. 'Are you ready for dinner?'

'I'll be along as soon as I've got my stuff out of the car.' He didn't suggest she waited for him. He didn't suggest they ate here, trying out the new kitchen and the adequately stocked fridge. It was dinner with the family.

'I'll tell them,' Daisy said. 'I'll see you later.'

Richard's car had been spotted, so they all knew he was back, and he followed her into the house within a few minutes, getting a welcome from everyone, dogs included. He hadn't changed his clothes. Why should he, now he wasn't playing a part any more, and this was how he dressed most of the time?

He brought gifts: a new pipe and a special brand of tobacco for Uncle Bob, a camera for Keith, a brooch for Nanny. For Alison there was a gold link bracelet, for Daisy three filigree daisies on a thin silver chain.

It was very pretty and she thanked him as they were all

doing, but she was not sure she would get much pleasure wearing a constant reminder of Richard. Even when her infatuation for him was well and truly over, and one of these days it must be, she might still be left remembering a wild and hopeless dream.

She was the only one who still wished she hadn't brought Richard here. Everyone else thought things had turned out perfectly. Richard had found a family, and somewhere he could escape and relax. He was telling them now that he had made arrangements to land his private plane about three miles away, on the old wartime American airstrip that was now used by a glider club, and that he hoped to get over most weekends.

He did just that. Sometimes he came by plane, sometimes by car, sometimes during the week he came without warning, and having a millionaire in the family caused hardly any upheaval at all.

He acquired a financial stake in the farm, and spent a lot of his time when he was at Oak House on the farm with Keith and Uncle Bob. Keith and Alison and Daisy and Richard went out for meals together now, it was a real cosy family set-up, and within a few weeks Daisy was beginning to pull herself together.

This was how it was going to be and she had to live with it. If she flung herself into Richard's arms he might accept the invitation, but he obviously preferred things as they were, without complications. This suited Richard and it had to suit Daisy.

Outwardly she bloomed, determined never to be caught sighing or showing signs of strain. She kept going, at work and at play, and when Richard was using the barn and sleeping next door she came home late, then read in bed until the words blurred and her eyelids were heavy as lead before she lay down and tried to sleep.

Nobody suspected how she felt, not even Alison, who was blithe as a lark again these days. Uncle Bob and Nanny had decided that Richard's life-style wasn't for Daisy, and it was better if he looked on her as a sister, another Alison. One day, they were both sure, Daisy would meet the right man.

Daisy was still inclined to be a little tart with Richard, amusing her family, amusing him. It seemed to Daisy these days that he acted as though she made up a trio with the dogs, another pet to be stroked and smiled at. Perhaps she was over-sensitive, but no one kept her as alert as Richard, and even when he was at his blandest she was always waiting for the barb somewhere.

She knew of course that he never gave her a second thought when they were apart. The press empire he ruled depended on his brilliance, stamina and commercial cunning, and while he was away from here he'd have no time to think about absent friends. It was another world.

On a shopping trip to London Daisy and Alison called in his office block—by appointment, of course—and Richard showed them around, introduced them to some of the staff, and took them out to lunch. It was all unreal to Daisy; the only thing remotely like it she had encountered had been on television, she was almost waiting for the plot to unravel.

Alison revelled in every minute of her day, shopping with gusto during the afternoon. She was a clever shopper, here for bargains, doing a hectic run of the big multiple stores down Oxford Street. She and Daisy always enjoyed their occasional day-excursions to London, and with Richard in the background this was turning into one of the most exciting outings Alison had ever had. She was so keyed up that she didn't notice how quiet Daisy was.

When their shopping was done they went back to the office to meet Richard again, and from there to his apartment. They were staying overnight this time, he was taking them to a theatre tonight, and then putting them up. And the penthouse flat, high over the lights of London, was something else out of television for Daisy.

No wonder he hadn't considered the barn palatial. Why

did he want the barn when he had a place like this? Daisy moved around stiffly, unable to relax, letting Alison do all the talking.

The play to which Richard took them was a smash hit, their seats were among the best, and altogether he did them proud; as Alison said when it was all over, and the sisters lay in twin beds, theatre programmes and half empty boxes of chocolates on the fitted dressing table.

Daisy agreed. After the theatre—dinner. And then a taxi back here, standing waiting for Richard to pick up his brief-case and suitcase to catch a midnight plane. He would get some sleep over the Atlantic, he said.

'I think it was very nice of him to spend this evening with us,' said Alison, sleepy and happy, 'when he's so busy, having to dash off to fly away.'

'Uh-huh,' murmured Daisy, sounding sleepy and happy too, and wondering cynically if that taxi would go to the airport—or if Richard had had enough of his country cousins and headed for more congenial female company overnight.

She wouldn't come here again. She tossed in the unfamiliar comfortable bed until Alison asked, 'Are you all right?' and then she said,

'I ate too much at dinner.'

'Me too,' said Alison. 'Wasn't it a fantastic place? I only hope poor Richard does get some sleep on that plane.'

'Poor Richard' should have made Daisy smile, but she wondered where Richard *was* sleeping tonight and wanted to cry ... Their cruising holiday was drawing near, and now the weather was cool, winter approaching, those islands in the sun should have beckoned like Shangri-La to Daisy.

They did to Alison, who could talk about nothing else these days, dreaming of a second honeymoon in romantic places and moonlit nights at sea.

Alison had been buying clothes for the cruise ever since it was decided they were definitely going and the route—

166

Madeira, Morocco, the Canaries—planned. So had Daisy, of course, but Alison was choosing her clothes like a trousseau, while Daisy's were just holiday gear.

At the end of November they would be flying out to Madeira, heading for the harbour where the boat was waiting, and Richard would be with them. He hoped to stay the whole of the trip, but with Richard there was always the chance he might have to fly away again to deal with some business matters. If he was there the romantic scenes and situations could be hazardous for Daisy. If he wasn't she would probably spend her time longing for him. Altogether she was much less eager to set sail than Keith and Alison were, and as she watched Alison gleefully crossing off the days on the kitchen calendar the narrowing remaining number really began to worry her.

It might be a fabulous holiday, a spellbinding adventure, but once aboard Richard's boat she didn't know what she might be sailing into.

With just over a week to go before their holiday Daisy was moving around some furniture in her living room, feeling like a change, when there was a rap on the wall between her and the barn. It sounded urgent. Both dogs began to bark, and she scrambled over the obstructing furniture to get out of the front door and hurry round to the barn, where Richard stood at the door.

The dogs went too, of course. 'Come in,' he said.

'Why were you knocking?' she asked.

'I wanted you round here.' There seemed no cause for panic, he could have come to her door whatever it was. He was walking across to his desk, and she saw then that he had the 'dark Lingard' papers. He must have collected them from the attic; the old leather suitcase she had put them in was on the floor, and he had been reading her manuscript. He sat down, a hand on the top page, and told her, 'You should finish this.'

'Why?' Now she knew his status in the journalistic world

167

it was embarrassing to have him inspecting her attempts at writing a book. In any case it was unpolished stuff, done for her own pleasure rather than publication, an account of her love affair with the dark Lingards.

'Because it might be worth finishing,' he told her.

This could be another pat on the head for the family pet. Daisy's little hobby that she hadn't touched since he came here. Any of the family—most likely Uncle Bob—could have suggested Richard looked at it, and got her working on it again. But that saga was finished; there were no more dark Lingards for her.

She looked ruefully at the pile of papers. 'I've outgrown fairy tales,' she said.

Richard gathered the papers together, put them into the yellow cardboard folder that had contained them and handed it to her. Daisy took it with a twisted smile because he was putting no pressure into persuading her to carry on, so he couldn't have thought much of the writing.

He said quietly, 'It's no masterpiece, but it has something,' and it was possible that no one had asked him to read it. He had asked her if he might, that night she and Alison had started their idiotic plan. When Daisy had admitted, 'I don't think it's very good,' Richard had said 'I'll be surprised if it isn't.' She would write no more about the dark Lingards, but if he thought her work had promise that was real encouragement. She gulped and asked, 'That's an honest opinion? You do think I can write?'

'Yes,' he said.

From the gallery came a low growl and a loud banging. Cooch had somehow negotiated the open steps of the staircase, and was now sitting up and bashing on a bedroom door with his front paws. 'Cooch,' shrilled Daisy, 'you stop that!'

The door opened, and Daisy had a fleeting glimpse of green dress, dark hair, white face. Then to her scream of 'Oh, my God!' the door shut again, and Cooch, bristling to twice his size, leapt at it.

Daisy dropped her yellow file, the papers spilling out, and ran for the stairs babbling, 'I'm so sorry—I'll get him. I didn't see him going up there. I didn't know there was anyone else here.'

Cooch, convinced he had an enemy cornered, was grinning with glee, bright eyes fixed on the closed door; and Woo was dashing around downstairs, barking like mad. Daisy clutched Cooch's mane as the door opened a fraction. 'Please don't come out,' she panted, dragging Cooch along the gallery.

'Don't worry about that.' The woman's voice followed her, and then, 'Is it a dog?'

'Sort of,' said Daisy.

At the top of the stairs she tried to push Cooch down, and he backed from the edge in affronted horror. 'You got up,' she hissed, 'you can get down!' but he baulked so stubbornly that she had to pick him up and carry him, and he lolloped in her arms, a ridiculous sight, so it was understandable that Richard was laughing as she reached ground level.

Daisy put Cooch on the floor, where he shook himself and continued to watch the door on the gallery, and said breathlessly, 'Sorry about that, I'll take them home. Do apologise for me, won't you?'

'I will,' said Richard.

Woo was still barking when she got back to the cottage. Both dogs had enjoyed themselves, both tails were wagging, and Daisy sat down on the nearest chair to the door. She felt weak as a kitten. All she wanted to do was crawl away and sleep for a hundred years. She had known that some time Richard would bring friends down here, but the girl next door with him now had drained the life out of her. She was numb and cold, and maybe it was as well she was. If she started to feel it was going to hurt like nothing had ever hurt her before.

She had known she would be jealous of any woman close to Richard, and there were probably plenty of them, and he might bring them all down here, some time or other, because he was a confirmed bachelor, a non-marrying man.

That might be easier than seeing Richard with a wife, so she should be glad he played the field, but she shrank from the thought of the pain ahead in the empty and desperate years that waited.

She replaced the furniture the way it had been before, and she had just finished when Richard knocked on the front door. She fastened Cooch in the kitchen, although she expected Richard to be alone from the way Cooch was wagging his tail, and when she opened the door she said, 'It's all right, I've caged him.'

Richard grinned. 'Funny you should say that. Louise thought he'd escaped from a zoo.'

'Do tell Louise how sorry I am that he frightened her,' said Daisy brightly. 'Oh, you brought my book.' He was holding the yellow cardboard file. 'Thank you, and thank you for saying you thought I could write. I'll carry on, if not with this with something else now I've had some encouragement from an expert.' She would, she supposed, but these were meaningless sounds she was making to fill the silence.

'Good,' said Richard. 'I'm taking Louise and George up to the house. Shall we see you there?'

She smiled, 'Without Cooch?' and Richard laughed.

'Louise isn't crazy about him. I had to come and check he was inside the cottage before she'd come out of the barn.'

Louise and George. Daisy's smile widened as soon as she was alone, because that sounded as though Louise and George belonged together. Please let the woman with the dark hair and the green dress, upstairs in one of Richard's bedrooms, belong to George. Please don't let her be Richard's love.

She was George's wife, which couldn't have suited Daisy

better, and they were a nice couple. George was middle size, with brown hair, neat moustache and beard, clever and cheerful, editor of one of Richard's newspapers, a friend who knew Richard well and thought there was no other man like him.

When Daisy arrived at Oak House George and Louise had already met the family, and everyone was chuckling over the story of Cooch charging the bedroom door. Louise and George, inside the room, had thought Richard was knocking, and Louise had answered the door because George was changing and trouserless.

'That dog's a menace,' said Nanny, who was very fond of Cooch but felt that somebody should be apologising for his bad manners.

'I am sorry about it,' Daisy assured them all, and George wiped his eyes, still chuckling.

'Lou squealed, "There's a wild animal out there!"' he told Daisy. '"A great hairy creature!"'

'She wasn't far wrong,' said Daisy. 'But I promise I'll keep him under control from now on.'

'A *pekingese*?' Louise sounded bewildered. 'He didn't look like a peke to me. But I'll take your word for it,' she added hastily. 'I'm keeping well away from him.'

It was a good-humoured start to their weekend visit. Daisy and Alison got on very well with Louise. The three young women were alone in the drawing room talking about the cruise, and Richard's boat—Lou and George had been on several trips—when Louise asked, 'Just you, is it? Just the family?'

There was a permanent crewman. With Richard that would be five aboard. 'He hasn't mentioned anyone else,' said Alison.

'Cassandra Mason's filming in Tenerife,' said Louise, 'so you could be picking her up.'

'Is she a friend of Richard's?' asked Alison, very impressed.

171

'Oh yes.' Louise was surprised they didn't know that. 'Keener on him than he is on her, but he's usually got some female in tow, hasn't he?'

Of course, Daisy could have said. Well, he would have, wouldn't he? A man couldn't be that eligible and not have the hopefuls milling around.

Daisy had no hope, but she had spirit and she met Alison's concerned glance with a grin, while she told Louise gaily, 'You're the first friends he's brought down here, we don't know too much about his private life, but he just has to be a ladykiller.'

'I wouldn't say that.' Louise wasn't sure now that she ought to say anything, because Richard *was* George's boss, and she *was* gossiping, but this was putting the record straight. 'Not a ladykiller,' she said firmly, 'he doesn't go hunting them.'

He doesn't need to, thought Daisy wryly. Louise added her own shrewd observation, 'And he makes quite sure they don't get any permanent ideas.'

Alison's eyes were still on Daisy, as though she was watching for Daisy's smile to falter, and Daisy said, 'Cassandra Mason! Imagine! We could be cruising with a famous actress. Is she as gorgeous in real life as she is on television?'

'She certainly is,' said Louise, then sighed and laughed, 'it isn't fair on us ordinary women, is it?' Cassandra Mason had long, long legs, and a golden-tanned body that could wear the briefest of bikinis. Her cloud of hair was pure deep rich amber, and Daisy could think of nothing more depressing than sharing a boat deck with Richard and Cassandra. Except, of course, the moment they walked away together.

As they would be sailing where she was filming, and she was such a close friend of Richard's, of course she would join the party, and that settled it for Daisy. She had been

172

worried about the cruise before, scared it might reduce her to one of his 'females in tow'. Now wild horses wouldn't have dragged her along.

She left it until the night before they were due to go before she told Alison. Any earlier would have given Alison more time for worrying, and possibly arguing. Alison and Keith were packed, and Daisy got Alison down to the cottage and said, 'I'm not coming.'

Alison had thought she was here to help Daisy finish her packing. She gasped and spluttered as though a bucket of cold water had been emptied over her. 'You're not—*what*?'

'I can't come,' said Daisy miserably. 'Not if we're picking up Cassandra Mason.'

Alison had believed Daisy was impervious to Richard's charm, and in the end been glad about that for Daisy's sake. But if Daisy couldn't go on this holiday, because of this girl-friend of Richard's, she must have been unhappy for weeks. 'You're not in love with Richard?' Alison whispered, as though it was a fearful secret that mustn't be spoken aloud.

'A little,' said Daisy. She was so much and so helplessly in love that she couldn't imagine ever being happy again, but she couldn't burden her sister with that on the eve of Alison's second honeymoon. 'Well, it isn't surprising,' Daisy babbled, 'because he is rather special. I shall get over it, of course, I know there's no future in it, but I shouldn't enjoy seeing him with a knockout girl like Cassandra Mason, and even if she didn't join us I'm not sure I mightn't make an awful fool of myself "once aboard the lugger", as the saying goes.'

Alison's heart was getting heavier and heavier. 'Oh Daisy!' she said at last. She had wanted Daisy in love, but safely, and there would be no security for a girl with Richard. She remembered Louise—'He makes sure they don't get any permanent ideas,' and all her protective instincts towards Daisy were roused. But all she could say was, 'Oh, Daisy!' again, and then, 'Oh dear, oh *damn*!'

'It is only a crush,' said Daisy, 'but it's the first crush I've had. Like getting measles late it's a shock to the system, but I'll get over it.'

She was twisting her hands together, lacing her fingers, but as Alison looked at her hands she realised how revealing this was and kept them locked and still. 'You won't say anything, will you?' she pleaded. 'Not even to Keith. I couldn't bear it if there was any chance of it getting to Richard.'

'*No*,' Alison promised in fierce reassurance. Daisy had hidden her feelings so convincingly because of her pride, and Alison would never do anything to hurt Daisy. She would never, *never* breathe a word of this. 'But how can you get out of coming now?' she wondered. 'We're as good as on our way.'

They were leaving early in the morning, and what excuse could Daisy give for staying behind at this stage? Daisy smiled wanly, 'A pity a crush doesn't bring you out in spots like measles. I've been praying all week that I'd go down with something that would lay me out but wasn't catching. I haven't, of course, but I think it will have to be one of those mystery bugs.'

Alison started listing the complications. 'They'll get the doctor, and take your temperature, and you know how Nanny is when you're sick, she'll know——'

'Leave that to me,' said Daisy. 'In the morning I can't travel. Maybe I'll have a raging migraine and bilious attack.'

Alison's lips parted, trying to get in a few more objections.

'But——' she began, but Daisy went on,

'It isn't as though I'll be letting anyone down. There are no deposits to be forfeited, and it won't make any real difference whether I'm there or not.'

'It *will*!' wailed Alison. 'It won't be half the fun if you're not there.'

'On your second honeymoon?' Daisy managed a grin. 'You and Keith won't need me around, and if Richard's got Cassandra Mason I would be the wallflower, wouldn't I? I'll stay here for a couple of days and then take myself off on a holiday somewhere. I'll——' She hadn't planned beyond tomorrow morning and she said the first thing that came into her head. 'I'll go touring the Highlands.'

'In *your* car, at *this* time of year?' shrilled Alison.

'Well, I'll go somewhere. And it isn't as though this is a once-in-a-lifetime thing, is it? I suppose Richard will let us go on his boat again. Next time I will go.'

'Will you?' Alison was seeking reassurance now, and Daisy said with a confidence she was far from feeling,

'Oh yes, I'll be over this in a month or two. But I can't face this trip, and you'll have to cover for me and tell them I couldn't travel, and say I'm doing something else with my holiday so there's no suggestion I could follow on later.'

Alison could see herself in a very awkward situation, but somehow she would cover for Daisy, without letting out the real reason why Daisy couldn't face what should have been a lovely holiday.

'Don't worry,' she said, 'I'll do it.' Daisy's eyes were bright with strain, although the light seemed to have left them. Hollows beneath the cheekbones changed the childish roundness of the face, turning prettiness into what would be a lasting beauty. But there was sadness, and Alison thought bitterly that heartbreak was a high price to pay for beauty. How could she leave Daisy like this? and she said, 'If you came you could—keep away from Richard. There'd be so much to see, to do. You needn't be alone with him, so you couldn't make a fool of yourself, and if this actress woman does turn up we could keep out of their way. Louise says it's a big boat.'

175

Daisy's face was impassive. 'No!' she was saying, without speaking, and Alison said desperately,

'I've been joking about second honeymoons, but you know that Keith and I want you along. It should be a super holiday and I know it would be better for you than moping around here. Oh, are you *sure* you can't come?'

'Oh yes,' said Daisy. Her hands were still clasped and her fingers ached. 'I'm sure all right,' she said.

She slept sounder that night than she had all week. The dream holiday had been a nightmare to her, but now at least the nightmare was lifted, that was one ordeal she didn't have to face. She slept heavily at first, but with dawn streaking the sky she waited for Alison and Keith, and began to worry that Alison might have confided in Keith, and he might have told Nanny, and the three of them might descend on her, telling her to stop behaving childishly.

That was what Nanny would say, although there was nothing childish about this. It was the woman in her, not the child, that was making a coward of her.

The dogs started barking and she heard Keith's car coming. Then she heard Alison call, 'Daisy? Ready?' and the rap on the door. A moment later the door opened with Alison's key, and Alison called again, 'Daisy? Where are you?'

'Up here,' Daisy called weakly back.

Alison came up the stairs and into the bedroom, shutting the door behind her, dropping her voice to ask, 'You're really going through with it?'

'Yes.'

'Oh dear! I'll have to go back and tell them, you know, otherwise nobody's going to believe you're ill.'

Daisy's excuse for not joining the party on Richard's boat must have credibility, and it was too late now for miracle cures, on a raging migraine-cum-bilious-attack, that would patch her up enough to get her on that plane. Daisy's

176

migraines were few and far between, but she had had the very occasional one and nobody could prove this was phoney.

All she had to do was imagine herself watching Richard and Cassandra Mason and she felt sick and her head did ache. It might be all in the mind, but she was incapable of getting up and getting into the car and driving off to the airport.

Telling Keith, 'Daisy's got a migraine, she can't move,' Alison went running back to the house, and Keith came running up the stairs, so concerned that Daisy's conscience pricked.

'What's this, then, old girl? You do look washed out. What rotten luck, today of all days.'

'Sorry,' said Daisy.

'Not your fault,' said Keith. 'We'll get you some aspirins, and you can lie down in the back of the car with the windows open. We'll get you there, don't you worry.'

Daisy turned her head on the pillow, and he patted her shoulder reassuringly. Then he went downstairs and looked out for Nanny and Alison, who came trotting down the track, straight past him and up the stairs. Keith said, as he followed them, 'We'll have to get a later plane.'

'No!' said Daisy sharply. 'If you cancel you'll upset all the arrangements, and I won't have that.' She was terrified that Keith was going to prove the stumbling block, re-adjusting the schedule or dosing her with medicines and carrying her to the car. She looked desperately at Alison, and Nanny, noting the flushed cheeks and the agonised tension, said,

'She'll be going nowhere today. Over-excitement, that's what it is. Brings on a bilious turn and a sick headache faster than anything, and they say it's next door to dying. Nothing for it but to lie quiet.' She crossed to the window, pulling the curtains close and shutting out the light.

Alison took Keith away, still protesting, and then ran back to kiss Daisy goodbye. 'You have a smashing time,' Daisy whispered.

'Yes,' said Alison.

'I am all right, you know.'

But Alison didn't believe her, and because of that Alison's holiday was going to be overcast. She was going to worry about Daisy, and Daisy wished she had had the strength to go on pretending. She might have done if it hadn't been for Cassandra. She felt miserable and ashamed, her opinion of herself at rock bottom.

When Alison and Keith had gone Nanny came in with an eau-de-cologne soaked handkerchief to lay on Daisy's forehead, and a lump of ice for her to suck to allay the sickness. 'I'm taking the dogs,' she said. 'You won't want them barking. Now you be still and get some rest and I'll be back.'

After that Daisy daren't get out of bed, and with the room in darkness, and nothing to be done for the next few hours, she fell asleep again. A too hasty recovery would have looked very odd. A migraine that totally incapacitated in the morning would at least last the day out, so Daisy passed a lazy day.

Nanny and Uncle Bob both came down to the cottage, commiserating with her on having missed her plane. It was going to be tricky explaining why she couldn't take another flight, but tomorrow she would announce her plans for an alternative holiday.

'I'm going to do some writing,' she would say. 'I've got this idea for a book, set in Cornwall. I'm going to a quiet hotel, on the coast somewhere.'

That was what she would do, and perhaps she would get an inspiration and start another book. Richard had said she could write. It was something, it was a great deal, to get the opinion of a man at the top.

Like the gifts he brought, Richard L. Judd offered her

help and encouragement. He was generous, often bringing things for his family. By the time she was an old woman Daisy could well have a lifetime's mementoes, starting with the Chinese lion and the filigree necklace. And the memory of the night he had taken her in his arms, and Woo had barked outside and Alison and Uncle Bob had come.

When she was old would she still remember, as she did now, the strong brown hands holding her, the delicate sensuality of his touch? If she had left with Keith and Alison today she would have been with Richard now, instead of alone in her cottage, wondering if she would be safe when she was old.

She was going to be alone tonight; the dogs were still at the house. 'After another night's sleep you'll be right as rain,' Nanny had promised. But as Daisy had slept most of the day she wasn't needing an early night, and she sat at the window, with a book on her knee, reading a little, but most of the time staring through the window at the grey world outside.

When she heard the plane going over she strained to catch sight of it, above the leafless trees. She couldn't see it in the patch of sky the window covered, but it sounded like Richard's plane. She knew the sound of that engine, at least she thought she did, and she put down the book and ran to the door, and the tiny dark speck was vanishing in the direction of the airstrip, although other private planes used that. Even if it was Richard's plane Richard didn't have to be in it. There was no reason why he should come back here tonight.

Except to fetch her, and he would probably do the same for Alison or Keith. 'Daisy-girl needs a holiday. Poor Daisy, going down with a sick headache. Like Nanny said, it would be over-excitement, like a child before a party.'

She couldn't go. She wouldn't. If it was Richard, if he did turn up, she'd say she'd already fixed another holiday.

She'd promised friends she would visit them. She'd promised to go somewhere with a friend. With Michael. She was still seeing him from time to time. She'd say she was falling in love with Michael and ... The sheer impossibility of that checked her whirling, panicking thoughts.

If it was Richard she simply did not know what she would do, but she couldn't sit here, waiting. She'd go for a little walk to cool her head. She needed fresh air, she had been cooped indoors all day, and waiting would be worse than coming back and finding it was not Richard's plane after all.

She grabbed a coat and ran down the track, and walked quickly in the opposite direction from the road that would bring a car from the airstrip, down towards the church, past the pub and the village green, into the lanes There were no footpaths here. She met no one, except when an occasional car passed her and she stepped on to the grass verge flanking the hedges.

She hadn't eaten a thing all day, you couldn't eat when you were supposed to be in the throes of a bilious attack and anyhow she had no appetite, so that her head felt muzzy. She was hardly marshalling her thoughts into logical order, rather she was getting herself into even more of a state, because if it was Richard she was in trouble, and if it wasn't she was going to be horribly disappointed.

Daisy didn't want to go on that cruise, but she badly wanted him to come and fetch her, and every time she heard a car coming along behind her she held her breath, letting it out in a sigh when the car passed by.

It was getting dark, soon she would have to go back. If Richard had been in that plane he would have reached Oak House a while ago, and certainly she couldn't expect him to be scouring the countryside for her. If he had come he would wait comfortably, either in Oak House or the barn.

She turned to turn back and the car rounding the bend

was Richard's. She just had time to replace her rapturous expression with a calmer look when the car drew up beside her. He leaned across to open the door on the passenger side. 'Can I give you a lift?' he asked.

Daisy stepped in, and he smiled down at her. 'I wonder if that's what Frederick said to his heiress? Frederick, the dark Lingard, scooping up the lady in his coach.'

Daisy laughed, 'Well, I'm no heiress, so no one's likely to kidnap me.'

Richard turned the car and they headed back for the village. 'I still think he didn't kidnap her,' he said. 'They eloped.'

'Maybe.'

'How are you?'

'Oh—better. Thank you.'

'Then we can leave tomorrow.'

It was so good sitting here beside him, this was the place she wanted to be, but Cassandra Mason's perfect face seemed to float between them and Daisy said jerkily, 'I can't. I've fixed to do something else now. I didn't think you'd come for me. I'm sorry I've been a nuisance.'

Richard appeared to agree heartily with her, although he said, 'Stop apologising.'

'Then stop bullying me! I tell you I can't come.'

'All right, all *right*.' He gripped the wheel for a moment as though he could have gripped her and shaken her, and they drove in silence through the silent village, and up the track to the farm. As Richard stopped the car in front of the cottage and the barn Daisy asked,

'Do they know you're here?'

'I went up there, when I found you weren't in.'

'How did you know I wasn't in bed, asleep?'

'The door wasn't locked, I went through all the rooms.'

'Be my guest,' she said.

'Don't be flip with me,' he grated, and she was nervous.

181

He was annoyed because she didn't look now as though she had been unable to move hand or foot this morning, and she was a nuisance, and she would have to go with him because she had no excuse that would stand up against his questioning. Except that she was so jealous of Cassandra that she would probably poison her before the trip was over. How was that for a reason for not going?

'What's the joke?' asked Richard.

Her lips must have twitched into a wry smile, and she said, meekly, 'I wasn't laughing.'

He opened the door of the barn, and took her arm, guiding her in. 'I've got some photographs to show you. Sit down and I'll get you a drink.'

She sat on the soft leather settee and said, 'Thank you, but I don't want a drink.'

'Well, I do.' He took a large brown envelope from one of the drawers of the desk, and put it beside her. Daisy opened it, afraid it might contain the photographs he had taken of her that Sunday, and it did.

She hardly noticed when he placed a glass on the table in front of her, nor that he stood with his own glass in his hand, watching her.

She remembered the day, these moments held for ever. She saw herself, just after the herd of cows had gone by, laughing: the pictures in the churchyard, by the river. Dozens of pictures, and the subtle change as the day wore on. This was a girl falling in love, until at last the words might as well have been spoken.

'I love you,' she was saying here in this last photograph, with the curve of her lips and the dreams in her eyes. She looked at each and set it aside, and felt her cheeks burning hot. With the last one she said, 'You *could* have been a professional photographer. You're very clever.'

'So are you,' he said, 'if that was acting.'

They left her exposed, vulnerable, and she couldn't deny them. She didn't know what to say.

He asked, 'Were you just setting me up for the evening performance for old Robert?'

Once she said, 'No,' she was in his hands. She said nothing and he said harshly, 'Look at me.'

He sat down beside her and she raised her eyes from the photograph of the smiling girl to the haggard face of the man, and saw how much it mattered to him and said, '*No*, of course I wasn't. It was a stupid idea and I hated it, and I forgot what I was supposed to be doing until I heard Woo barking. I went to pieces. I was shaken out of my wits, and that's the truth.'

Richard's voice was quiet, constrained, 'Then why have you kept me at arm's length ever since?'

If she answered that she was beyond recall. He shifted slightly and instinctively she drew back and he said drily, 'I won't touch you, you don't need to jump away.'

'I wasn't.' A small lie, but she hadn't meant to shrink from him.

'If you don't it will make a change,' he said. 'I'm not a plague-carrier nor a sex maniac. Contact with me should leave you unscarred.'

'Should it?' She sounded doubtful, and he sighed and said,

'Oh, God, what *is* wrong? Why wouldn't you go with Alison and Keith? It would have been a good holiday, it's a good boat, and I'd hoped we might reach an understanding where the atmosphere was more relaxed.'

That didn't sound as though Cassandra would be around, and it was an admission that Richard still wanted her. She could take her happiness, sailing away to blue seas and blue skies, but she remembered how she had felt when she believed that Louise was Richard's lover, and this was no simple question of morality.

Once she went to Richard if he turned away from her it would kill her. To survive she must stay behind her defences. She said huskily, 'I think it would take more

183

than a relaxing atmosphere to bridge the gulf between us.'

'What gulf?' He looked down at the photographs. 'There was no gulf that day.'

That day they had been drawn together in mind and body and Daisy had thought it was the beginning of a closeness in which they would be inseparable. 'You were Richard Lingard then,' she said. 'Now you're Richard Judd.'

'So?' He sounded as though he didn't know what she was talking about, but it meant that, while she loved him alone, to him she would only be one of many. With her head bowed, so that he couldn't read her eyes, she said,

'What do you want me for?'

'To share with,' he said. 'To laugh with. To argue with. To love.'

That was how she wanted it to be and that was what he was offering her now. You couldn't claim the future, maybe you shouldn't try, but she heard herself ask, 'For how long?'

'Until I close my eyes for the last time,' he said, and she raised her head then and looked at him. His face could have been carved, eyes hooded, the line of mouth hard and straight, but the tiny muscle moved in his cheek, and her fingers reached to touch it, to stroke gently.

He put up a hand and pressed her fingers against his face and told her, 'Since I knew you I haven't wanted to touch another woman, much less make love to one. There would never be another after you.'

Daisy believed him. He was speaking from the heart. 'When I told Robert I wanted to marry you I was angry enough to murder you, but it was still the truth. I did want to marry you. I'd have asked you that night, and told you about myself, if there'd been no interruptions.'

'You would?' she whispered.

'What would you have said?'

Her voice was lilting with love and laughter. 'Anything, I think,' she said. 'From what I remember you were sweeping me off my feet.'

His laugh was a caress and she was in his arms, her lips parting to receive his kiss. After a long moment, his lips still on hers, he said, 'What gulf?'

'I think we've bridged it,' she mumbled.

'What would you have said?'

'Are you asking me to marry you?'

'Yes.'

'Yes.'

His arms around her tightened until she could hardly breathe. 'Tell me you love me,' he said.

'I'll always love you.'

'I love you, Daisy Penrose. Daisy Penrose Lingard Judd,' the crooked smile, that she had recognised and loved from the first moment she saw him. He was looking at her now as though she was all he would ever want. 'I miss you when you're not with me,' he said. 'I need you. I've always missed and needed you, even before I met you. Does that make any sense?'

'All the sense in the world.' Tomorrow they would catch the plane and fly out to the boat. Cassandra wouldn't be coming aboard, but it wouldn't matter if they met her. Not now. Not ever. She said, 'Alison will be surprised.'

'Will she?' He grinned. 'When I said I was coming back for you she said, "Good luck, then".' His fingers played with her hair. 'What about giving her a real surprise?' he said. 'I do have a special licence. What about getting married right away, and there's this little island they'll be calling at. We could be sitting on the beach waiting for them, an old married couple.'

'That sounds lovely.'

She wanted to marry him as soon as she could. She

ached to be his wife, to have him for her lover, her husband, her friend. He drew her face closer to his face, fingers entwined in her hair, and she melted against him and then—like the last time—she heard it.

Richard's expression was comical disbelief. 'Do you hear what I hear?'

'Woo,' she said. 'Somebody's coming to see if you found me. Either Uncle Bob or Nanny, or possibly the pair of them.'

He burst out laughing, kissed her, and they were both laughing. 'This time,' he said, 'we have real news for them.'

Now available!

COLLECTION EDITIONS

of Harlequin Romances

Harlequin is proud to present this collection of the best-selling romance novels of former years. This is a rare series of 100 books, reissued in beautifully designed new covers. And the cost is only 75¢ each. See complete listing on accompanying pages.

Not sold in stores.

Harlequin Collection Editions

Please note: The number in brackets indicates the original Harlequin Romance number.

Harlequin Collection Editions

Please note: The number in brackets indicates the original Harlequin Romance number.

Harlequin Collection Editions

Please note: The number in brackets indicates the original Harlequin Romance number.

Harlequin Collection Editions

Please note: The number in brackets indicates the original Harlequin Romance number.

Complete and mail this coupon today!